BUT NOT
FOREVER

A CLINT WOLF NOVEL
(BOOK 4)

BY

BJ BOURG

WWW.BJBOURG.COM

TITLES BY BJ BOURG

STAND-ALONE YA MYSTERY

The Seventh Taking

MAGNOLIA PARISH MYSTERY SERIES

Hollow Crib   *Hollow Bond*

LONDON CARTER MYSTERY SERIES

James 516   *Elevation*
Proving Grounds   *Blood Rise*
Silent Trigger   *Rapture*
Bullet Drop   *Murderfield*

CLINT WOLF MYSTERY SERIES

But Not Forgotten   *For But Not Fame*
But Not Forgiven   *But Not Forthcoming*
But Not Forsaken   *But Not For Justice*
But Not Forever   *But Not For Wrath*
But Not For Naught
But Not Forbidden
But Not Forlorn
But Not Formidable
But Not For Love
But Not Forborne
But Not Forewarned
But Not Foreboding
But Not Forespoken
But Not For Blood
But Not Foreknown
But Not Fortuitous
But Not For Fear
But Not Foreseen
But Not For Lust
But Not Forspent
But Not Forsworn
But Not Foregone
But Not For Vengeance
But Not Foregathered
But Not Foredoomed
But Not Foretold
But Not Forfeited
But Not Forearmed

BUT NOT FOREVER
A Clint Wolf Novel by BJ Bourg

This book is a work of fiction.
All names, characters, locations, and incidents are products of the
author's imagination, or have been used fictitiously.
Any resemblance to actual persons living or dead, locales, or events
is entirely coincidental.

Cover design by Christine Savoie of Bayou Cover Designs

PUBLISHED IN THE UNITED STATES OF AMERICA

CHAPTER 1

3:25 p.m., Monday, September 26
Dire Lane, Mechant Loup, Louisiana

"Cindy, this is my friend, Kegan Davis," Burton Vincent told his younger sister as he and Kegan stepped out of his room and into the hallway. "Kegan, this is my adopted sister, Cindy."

Having heard the joke a million times, Kegan adjusted the backpack on his shoulder and chuckled, but Cindy wasn't amused.

"Don't take my word for it—just look at her," Burton continued. "She's got red hair and green eyes while my mom, dad, and I all have brown hair and brown eyes. Either she's an alien or she's adopted." Burton pretended to see the lanky kid standing behind Cindy for the first time. "Who the hell are you and how'd you get in my house?"

"Shut up, Burt." Cindy pushed by Burton and waved her boyfriend along, her eyes boring into Burton as she did so. "Come on, Troy. Don't pay attention to my idiot brother."

Cindy had been dating Troy Gandy for a few months and this was the first time she'd invited him over—and Burton wasn't happy about it. His parents weren't home and, although he brought girls to the house all the time when they were gone, he didn't like his sister doing the same. Troy started to move around Burton and Kegan, but Burton blocked his way. At seventeen, Burton was a year older than Troy and towered over him.

"My dad bought me a gun and he told me to shoot any boy who goes in my sister's room. You're not going in her room, are you?"

Troy's lower lip twitched just a little. "Um, I'm going

with...um...we're going study in her...um...we're going to—"

"You'd better stay out of her room." Burton's eyes narrowed. "She might be adopted, but we love her like she was our blood."

"Come on, Troy!" Cindy bellowed from the end of the hallway. "Don't even talk to him."

Troy hesitated and Burton seized upon it. "Don't you do it, little man. I've got the green light from my dad and I'll take you out."

"Maybe we should...um...hang out in..."

"Troy, he's lying. He's a liar. My dad wouldn't trust him with a gun if he was forty. Now get in here!"

Burton fixed Troy with a cold stare and slowly shook his head.

"If you don't stop," Cindy warned, pointing a finger at Burton, "I'm telling Dad you set the neighbor's hay bales on fire."

"Hey, that was an accident! That bottle rocket was defective."

Cindy reached around Burton and grabbed Troy's arm, dragging him past her brother. They disappeared in Cindy's room, but before the door was shut, Burton yelled, "Cindy, that football player called again and said he wants to take you back to the movies. He said he loves you!"

Cindy cursed Burton from her room. Although the door was shut, he heard her plainly.

Kegan broke out laughing. "You're an ass! That was the coolest thing I've ever seen!"

Burton clenched his fists. "I hate that little dude. I heard he walks around school bullying the smaller kids."

"Did you tell Cindy?"

"She doesn't want to believe it. She thinks he's the best thing since Facebook."

. "Beat his ass—but only use your left hand so it'll be a fair fight."

"My mom said if I get in another fight she's pulling me out of football."

"Really? If my mom told me that, I'd punch her right in the face."

"What?" Burton stared incredulously at Kegan. "You wouldn't dare hit your mom."

"Wanna bet? That would be considered a fight and if that's what it took for her to let me quit football, I'd do it in a heartbeat. I hate football more than I hate mosquitoes."

Burton shook his head idly and stared at Cindy's bedroom door, then turned back to Kegan.

Kegan was shorter than Burton; his complexion was darker and he had longer hair, too. Of course, it wasn't hard to be darker than Burton. He was so pale his friends called him "Whitemare" on the football field. He was six foot and weighed in at one-seventy, but it was a solid one-seventy. When he hit opposing linemen, they felt it. Kegan, on the other hand, was a little over five feet and barely clocked in at one-forty with his uniform and helmet on.

As Burton stared down at his friend, Kegan's pimply face broke out into a full grin. "What do you think Cindy and that dude are doing?"

"They'd better not be doing anything," Burton said, scowling. "He probably doesn't even like her."

"I don't know. She's kinda pretty."

"Dude, shut the hell up!" Burton punched Kegan's shoulder playfully. "That's the sickest thing you've ever said—and you say some sick stuff."

Kegan chuckled quietly and tiptoed to Cindy's door, pressing his ear against it. "I think they're having sex," he whispered.

Burton's blood instantly boiled. He stepped into his room and snatched up the chair from his desk. He then placed it across the floor at the far end of the hall, where it was dark and hard to see, and strode to Cindy's room.

Taking a deep breath, he tried the doorknob. It was locked. He immediately smashed his fist against the door and bellowed, "Dude, you'd better put your clothes back on and get the hell out of here! My dad's home early and he's got a gun!"

A high-pitched shriek sounded from inside the room—it wasn't Cindy's voice—and was followed by frantic bumping and rustling. The door opened a second later and Troy raced from the room carrying his shoes. He crashed into the chair and screamed as he pitched forward. He landed with a thump, his shoes flying through the air. One of them smashed into a picture frame on the wall, breaking it and causing glass to rain down onto the floor. Troy scrambled to his feet, gathered his shoes, and then scurried out the front door.

Cindy stormed over to where Kegan and Burton stood laughing and shoved a finger in Burton's face. "You're an asshole! That's it—I'm tired of keeping your dirty little secret. You're going to jail for arson!"

Before Burton could reply, she turned on her heels and returned to her room, shoving the door shut and locking it.

Still laughing, the boys walked outside and headed toward the back of the street. "Let's go see if Paulie wants to mess with some alligators," Burton said.

Paul Rupe lived a few blocks down the street, and his was the last house down Dire Lane. Paul was as tall as Burton, but not as physically fit. He preferred playing video games while Burton and Kegan favored contact sports, but all three loved fishing and harassing alligators.

When they reached Paul's house, Burton and Kegan rushed up the wooden steps and banged on the door. It didn't take much to convince Paul to come along with them, and the three boys were soon heading toward the canal west of the neighborhood, which was appropriately named Westway Canal.

The sun was shining brightly and, although it was supposed to be fall, it felt like the middle of summer. Burton knew it would be cooler once they reached the trees, but they had to first cross about five hundred yards of grassy fields. As they trudged through the thick weeds their shoes kicked up pollen from the foliage and Paul began to sneeze.

"Damn it," he mumbled. "I should've brought some Benadryl."

"You're lucky you don't play football," Burton said. "Some of those guys spend the whole time miserable—sneezing constantly, snot dripping from their noses. It's disgusting."

"Trust me…it ain't like we sneeze on purpose just to gross you out."

"You could control it if you wanted to," Kegan chided. "You're just being difficult."

The three boys laughed and pressed on. When they finally reached the wooded area behind the neighborhood, Kegan slipped the backpack off his shoulder and removed a primitive tomahawk from inside. It was made of wood and stone and held together with leather straps. He hefted it in one hand. "This is the best gift anyone ever gave me, Paulie. If something attacks us, we'll be ready."

Paul had given Kegan the tomahawk last month when his family returned from vacation. Still more than a little jealous, Burton grunted. "Yeah, and all I got was a shitty piece of paper."

"It wasn't just a piece of paper," Paul said, dipping under a low-lying tree branch and scurrying down the bank to the edge of the canal. He stopped just short of the water and waited for Burton and Kegan to join him. "By the way, what'd you do with it?"

"I stuck it on the refrigerator door with one of those magnets my mom has, but it disappeared two days later. No one has claimed responsibility, but I know Cindy did it." Burton shrugged. "If it would've been a tomahawk, maybe I'd care, but it was just a stupid—"

"Hey, what the hell is that?" Paul's shrill cry cut Burton's sentence short.

Burton slid down the embankment and skidded to a stop beside Paul and Kegan. Paul was pointing to the opposite side of the canal about a hundred yards north of their position, where the water was low from the outgoing tide. Much of the opposite edge of the canal was exposed and something was plopped onto the mud a few feet from the bank.

"Whatever it is," Burton said, shielding his eyes from the sun, "it looks like it got stranded when the tide went out. Let's move closer."

Burton led the way along the water's edge. His feet sank into the soft mud as he walked and water seeped into his shoes. On a normal day, he didn't like walking around in wet socks, but he hardly noticed. His eyes were focused on the object and his mouth began to widen as they neared the area directly across the canal from it.

"Is that…?"

"Damn, dude!" Kegan's fingers dug into Burton's shoulder as he tried to push his way around his friend. "That's a dead body!"

CHAPTER 2

It was a little before five o'clock when I passed up my driveway and stopped abruptly to back my boat trailer under the carport. Achilles, my jet black German shepherd, lurched forward on the seat beside me and almost spilled onto the floor. He righted himself and then looked at me as though to say, "Next time you decide to stop suddenly, how about a warning first?"

I laughed and reached over to rub his thick neck. He licked my hand and scooted closer to me. He was over a hundred pounds and took up most of the seat, but I didn't mind. He was a good friend and a fierce protector. The tourists loved him more than they loved me and nearly everyone would mention him by name in their online reviews.

I backed my boat into its normal spot and shut off the engine. Achilles didn't even wait for me to open the door. He bounded through the front window and headed for the back yard at breakneck speed, barking as he ran. I shook my head. He had probably seen another squirrel and would chase it up a tree and then spend the rest of the evening wondering how to get up there after it.

My fiancée, Police Chief Susan Wilson, wasn't home, and I began to wonder if she'd miss training again. She and I had each sold the houses we'd owned separately and built this nice home together. Complete with a thirty-by-thirty gym, it was located at the beginning of Paradise Place. We both agreed it would be better to remain close to the shelter, which was at the end of Paradise Place, where we could handle any issues that might arise. Being at this location, we would know anytime someone came or went, and we were close enough to keep the women and children who stayed with us safe.

I stepped out of my truck and walked to the edge of the paved carport, where I stomped the mud from my rubber boots. I was about to kick them off when tires screeched behind me. I turned to see Susan speeding up the driveway in her marked Chevy Tahoe.

"Don't take those off," she said when she stepped out of the driver's seat and walked briskly toward me. "I'm going to need you."

Loving the sound of that, I leaned against the wooden post at the corner of the carport and admired her as she drew closer. A tan polyester uniform never looked so good. It wasn't tight, but was snug enough to reveal the hardened body beneath it. Her gun belt rose and fell with the sway of her hips and her powerful legs tested the fabric of her pants. The muscles in her bronze-colored arms flexed when she reached up and pushed the dark shades high up on her forehead, revealing her dark eyes.

"You need me? Or want me?" I asked when she was close enough for me to detect specks of paint in her brown hair. As she always did when she was working or fighting, she'd braided her hair into cornrows and tied them off into twin pigtails. I reached up and scratched at the paint, but stopped when she leaned up to kiss me. At five-eight, she was only two inches shorter than me.

"I always want you," she said with a smile after pulling away, "but I also need you right now. Some boys found a body grounded on the western bank of Westway Canal. I need a boat to take me there and, since you're my favorite captain, you get the pleasure of bringing me."

I eyed her suspiciously. Over the past year she'd been okay with my decision to leave police work, but since the work on the shelter was nearly complete and I wouldn't be as busy, she began hinting at my return to the police department.

"Last I checked, the Mechant Loup Police Department owned several boats," I said slowly. "And you can drive all of them. So...do you really want me for my boat, or do you want me to have a look at the dead body?"

Susan shoved her fists into her hips and frowned. "You know how it's sometimes necessary to force-feed a dead rat to a snake that stops eating?"

I nodded slowly, not knowing where she was going.

"Well, I figured if I'd force-feed a dead human to you, you'd want to get back into homicide investigations."

"Wait—do you think it's a homicide?"

"Nah, it's probably just another drowning," Susan's face brightened up and she stabbed at my chest with her finger, "but did you notice how excited you got there? You want to come back, I just know you do."

Frowning, I explained—yet again—that I'd lost the right to wear a badge when I did what I did last year. "It was dishonorable."

"You were cleared of any wrong doing. It was a justified shooting."

I opened my mouth to argue, but she pushed her fingers against my lips.

"The people in this town need you, Clint Wolf. Who are you to deny them?"

We'd had this discussion before, where I'd tried a different tack, saying it wouldn't be proper for me to work for my future wife. "It wouldn't be ethical," I'd argued.

"I've already spoken with Mayor Cane and she cleared it with the ethics board," Susan had countered. "She'll hire you as the town investigator and you'll work directly for her, same as me, and there'll be no issues with nepotism. We'll be separate, but co-equal, branches of the town government. I'll be the chief of police and you'll be the chief of detectives—only you won't have any other detectives under you."

She had laughed at the last part and I'd only grunted.

Not wanting to rehash the argument now, I grunted again, but trudged to my truck. "I'll take you to the body, but only because I love you—not because I want to work cases again."

Giving a triumphant yell like she did when she wins a cage fight, she hurried to her Tahoe and backed out the driveway, heading for the boat launch. I checked on Achilles—he was still trying to figure out how to get up the tree—and closed the gate to lock him in the back yard. After getting back in my truck and firing up the engine, I pulled out of the driveway and headed toward Main Street.

While I didn't want to admit it out loud, there was a surge of adrenalin running through me as I sped down the highway. It felt like the good old days, when I would rush out to a death scene, wondering what I'd find when I arrived. One thing was certain about death investigations—no two scenes were the same and no two cases were alike. There might be similarities, but there was no such thing as identical cases.

The sun was sinking low and shining directly in my eyes as I made my way down Main Street. I shoved the visor down and glanced to my left as I drove by the barren concrete foundation that used to be the police department. I remembered well the gun battle that had ensued there, rocking the quaint little town to its roots, and robbing us of some fine people—civilians and officers.

As I reflected on that fateful day, the raw feelings of fear, loss, and rage came pouring back over me. My heart began to pound as though I was back in the moment…bullets whizzing by, people screaming, ears ringing. Although I'd come very close to death during that shootout, I suddenly realized I felt more alive back then than I did just now.

I sighed. Maybe Susan was right. If the town needed me, who was I to deny them? Besides, I probably needed them more than they needed me. Giving swamp tours was a great gig and it was fun being out on the water and meeting people from all over the world. But, deep down, that's not who I was and I couldn't be a swamp guide forever. I was a cop. I was meant to do the job.

CHAPTER 3

A cool breeze was blowing off of Bayou Tail and droplets of water rained down on us intermittently as the front of my boat rocked up and down when we hit waves from other boat traffic. My mind raced faster than the boat was traveling, wondering what we would find once we arrived at the scene. A body on the water held many possibilities, most of which involved drowning, but something nefarious could also be amiss. I felt alert. Excited, even. While I didn't like the fact that people had to die, I was passionate about resolving death investigations. If it turned out to be a homicide, I would be doing God's work, because homicide investigators work for God.

"I'll do it," I said, raising my voice to be heard above the noise of the wind and the boat motor.

"Do what?" Susan asked, leaning closer.

"I'll take the job as the town investigator."

Susan gave a bounce for joy and hooked her arm under mine, causing me to jerk the steering wheel to the right. She quickly let go and I righted the boat. We both began to laugh. She appeared as relieved as I felt.

"Thank you so much!" She was beaming. "It'll take a load off of me. What with the everyday chief duties, trying to get the shelter in order, and training for my fight with Antonina Ivanov"—she shook her head—"the last thing I need right now is a death investigation."

I frowned. As Susan racked up the wins in her mixed martial arts career—she had twelve wins, zero losses—the competition became tougher...and Ivanov was as tough as they came. The Russian champion was undefeated in her mixed martial arts career, as well as in her career as a professional boxer. Rumor had it she even fought men in Russia—and she'd never lost. It was going to be her first fight on American soil and we had no idea what to expect. I had faith in Susan, but I was also worried about her.

"Whatever I can do to help, Love," I called back, trying to conceal the worry I felt as I turned right onto Westway Canal. Her fight was a month away, so I pushed it from my thoughts and concentrated on the task at hand.

Westway Canal was narrower than Bayou Tail, but it was still about fifty feet wide. It was lined on both sides by dense forestland. The trees would open up in places to cow pastures or patches of marshland, but those were narrow strips of land. We'd had a few weeks of dry weather and the tide was lower than usual, exposing the soft mud at the edges of the bayou.

We had traveled about a mile when Susan pointed toward our right. "Look, there're some boys at the edge of the canal. They must've called it in."

The boys were immersed in the shadows of the live oaks and bald cypress trees that littered the bank of the canal, and it was hard to make them out until we idled closer to their location. I couldn't reach the bank because of the shallow water, so I cut off the engine when we were close enough to make contact. Two of the boys were tall—had to be six foot each—and the other was shorter. One of the taller boys was muscular and the other appeared weakly, while the shorter one was average build.

"I'm Chief Wilson," Susan announced, waving her hand in the direction of the boys. "Which one of you called it in?"

The more muscular of the tall boys raised a hand. "I did."

"What's your name?" Susan asked.

"Burton Vincent." After identifying his buddies as Paul Rupe (the weakly one) and Kegan Davis (the short one), he pointed across the canal. "We think there's a body over there in the mud."

Susan nodded and we both looked where he pointed. I used a hand to shield my eyes from the setting sun and squinted against the brilliance. Sure enough, there was a humanoid figure lying in a supine position in the soft mud near the opposite bank.

"How long ago did—"

"Burton, are you okay? What's going on down there?" called a masculine voice from the trees above where the boys were standing, cutting off Susan's question. "Your mom said you found a dead person."

Susan and I turned our attention to the man, who wore khaki

slacks and a button-down dress shirt. He was picking his way down the embankment toward the boys, trying not to slide in the soft grass.

"Yeah," Burton called, waving his dad forward. "It's down here, across the canal."

The man ducked under a low-lying branch and stood beside the boys. He was shorter than Burton and a little heavier. A green leaf was stuck to his thick brown hair and Burton laughed as he removed it.

"Where is it?" the dad asked, directing his question toward Susan. "I'm Rick Vincent, by the way. I'm Burton's father. Is it a real body?"

Susan nodded and pointed toward the location. "Your son and his friends made quite a discovery. Once we're done here, we'll need to take a formal statement from them."

The man nodded. "Sure, absolutely."

"Can we watch?" asked Kegan.

Susan cocked her head sideways. "I can't make y'all leave, but we'll be here for a few hours processing the scene."

"We don't mind waiting," Paul said, his eyes wide with excitement. "I've never seen a dead person before."

"No, boys," said the elder Vincent. "We'll head back to the house and wait for them."

"Before you head out," Susan said, turning her attention to the boys, "who was the first to spot the body?"

"Paul saw it first, but Kegan was the first to realize it was a body," Burton said.

"What'd y'all do next?"

"I called nine-one-one and then I called my mom and told her what we found," Burton explained. "It was kind of scary. We've never seen a dead body before and we didn't know what happened and—"

"But we were ready," Kegan interrupted, lifting a tomahawk in his hand. "If someone would've shown up to start trouble, we were prepared."

I turned my head away so they wouldn't see me grinning. Susan thanked them and asked for their addresses and a contact number. "If it's too late when get done out here, I'll swing by in the morning. Or"—I felt her staring at me—"our new investigator will be in touch."

After telling Susan where each of the boys lived and providing her with his cell number and the numbers of Kegan and Paul's parents, Rick ushered the boys up the embankment and they disappeared into the deep shadows of the forest. The boys were grumbling out loud and questioning why they had to leave.

"Because that's official police business and it's none of our business," Rick said, but the boys were having none of it. They grumbled until they were out of earshot.

"Is that what we have to look forward to if we have boys?" Susan asked.

I cranked up the boat motor and grunted. "Let's hope we never have a son like me."

"And why's that?" Susan rested her hand against the side of the boat as I guided it gently toward the opposite side of the canal, careful not to disrupt the water much.

"I gave my mom fits. I climbed every tree I could find—the taller the better—and would hang upside-down from the highest branches."

"How'd you do that?"

"I'd throw my legs over the branches and just hang there." I eased back on the throttle as the front of the hull scraped the soft mud about ten feet from where the body had been marooned. "I'd also climb our house and the neighbors' houses just to jump off."

Susan's eyes were on the body, but she was listening to me, and shook her head. "You're right...I don't want a son like you."

I killed the engine and watched as Susan grabbed the push pole and tested the mud. "It's too soft to walk on. We'll sink to our waist in this mud."

"What do you want to do, Chief?" I asked, enjoying my last day of freedom.

"I'll call Melvin and have him bring some creosote boards out here so we can make a bridge around the body."

While she made the call, I leaned forward and looked toward the body, wondering what it would tell us.

CHAPTER 4

Forty minutes later...

I looked up when the roar of the airboat sounded from the south but had to wait another ten minutes before Melvin Saltzman came into view. He was perched atop the elevated captain's seat and wore dark glasses and thick earmuffs.

Melvin was my height, but weighed two-fifty. His face was thick and tanned and it immediately lit up when he saw me. He killed the engine and allowed the airboat to drift in our direction. He dropped down from the captain's seat and tossed a rope in our direction. I tied it to my boat while he eased an anchor into the water.

Once he straightened, he stripped the earmuffs from his smooth head and smiled big. "Damn good to see you again, Chief." He cocked his head to glance past me at Susan. "And you, too, Chief."

"Stop calling me that," I said for the millionth time. Even though I'd been gone for a year, he still called me "chief" every time he saw me.

He shrugged. "It's a habit now, and I like the way it rolls off my tongue."

I leaned across the water that separated my boat from his and shook his hand. "Well, it's always good to see you, too."

Melvin looked toward the body and frowned. "What do you think happened to him?"

"Hard to say from here," I said, "but he's definitely been in the water for a while."

"Do you think he floated in from Bayou Tail?" Melvin asked.

"It's a thought." From where we were positioned, I could tell he'd been in the water for several days. His stomach had swelled to the point that it had popped the buttons on his purple button-down shirt. The skin around his mouth and nose had been gnawed away by marine life and one arm was folded at a ninety-degree angle at the elbow and was suspended in the air, held there by rigor mortis. Since rigor mortis could remain fixed for up to seventy-two hours, it was possible we were looking at a three-day window of death.

Below the swollen belly, the man wore a pair of blue jeans. The fabric around the waist was taut and it looked like the flesh was about to rip. The fronts of both pant legs were dry from exposure to the hot sun, but the groin area and the entire back of the jeans were still wet. There was a belt around his waist that bore a fancy buckle, but I couldn't identify what it was from my position.

The man's left shoe was missing, but there was a white sneaker on his right foot. His left foot was covered by a white sock, but it looked like the sock was barely hanging on. To me, it appeared the shoe had been ripped off and it almost took the sock with it. *What did it mean?* At that time, I had no clue.

Knowing the body had floated here, we didn't have to worry much about our approach to the scene. Melvin moved to the port side of the airboat and removed a ten-foot plank from the narrow space beside the bench seats. He carefully guided it in my direction and I took it from him. Susan and I then slid the plank forward until it was near the left side of the body. We took the next plank and slid it toward the right side of the body.

"Do you think it'll hold our weight?" Melvin asked.

"Only one way to find out," Susan said, stepping out of the boat and slowly putting her weight onto the board on the left. It sank about an inch, pushing up black water and releasing marsh gas, but then it stopped. She shrugged. "Looks like I'm okay."

After handing Susan the crime scene box she'd taken from her Tahoe when we were at the boat launch, I went next, placing one boot at a time on the board and slowly lowering my weight onto it. My board sank a little more than Susan's, but it held. I twisted at the waist and reached out as Melvin handed me another board, which we laid across our two boards and slid forward until it was directly beside the body. Getting on her hands and knees, Susan crawled out over the cross-board and began visually examining the body.

Since I wasn't officially a part of the police department yet, I mainly handed her things—the camera, several pairs of gloves, swabs for DNA samples, bags to cover the victim's hands, and on and on—and offered bits of advice when she asked for it.

After thoroughly examining the front of the body, she glanced over at me. "I don't see any signs of trauma. You?"

The sunlight was waning and mosquitoes were already out in full force. I wiped sweat from my brow and shook my head. "Nothing that I can see."

Susan asked Melvin to turn on his spotlight and aim it at the body. Next, she asked him to throw us the body bag.

Once we had it, we unzipped it and stretched it out over the cross-board beside the victim's body. I pulled on a pair of latex gloves and scooted to the end of my board, which was near his head.

Susan grabbed his feet and glanced up at me. "Ready?"

I nodded and she counted down from three. On *one*, we both rolled him over and guided him over the body bag. We had to force his arm straight to get it in the body bag. Once he was positioned on his face, Susan turned her attention toward his back.

"Oh, shit!" she said when she took in the back of his shirt. "This is a homicide."

She was right. There were six bullet holes in the back of the man's shirt. While the fabric was wet and muddy, we could still make out blotches of red where blood had oozed from the wounds.

After Susan photographed the outside of the shirt, she gently lifted it so we could examine the bullet wounds. The shot pattern wasn't remarkable. There was a sixteen-inch spread between the farthest two wounds, with the other four scattered within that area and no two holes were closer than five or six inches apart. An average cop could easily fire that size of a group from twenty-five yards, but I didn't know what type of training our killer possessed—if any. As far as I could tell, there was no fouling or stippling on the shirt, so the shots were fired from several feet away.

"Depending on our shooter's proficiency with firearms, the victim was shot from as little as three feet and as much as several yards away," I said. "Judging by the lack of penetration depth and the size of the wound, I'd guess a small caliber handgun was used—maybe a .38 or .380."

"If I had the authority," Susan said, "I'd swear you in right now—out here on the water, with God, the dead guy, and Melvin as our witnesses." Susan straightened on her knees and glanced up and down the canal, frowning as she shook her head. After a year of peace in Mechant Loup, this was the last thing she wanted—or needed.

"What are you talking about?" Melvin called from behind us. "Who's getting sworn in?"

Susan and I looked at each other, and then turned to stare at Melvin, who waited like an eager child, leaning over the edge of the airboat with his mouth open. When neither of us spoke, he stomped his foot in feigned protest. "What's going on?"

Susan turned her attention back to the body. "You tell him."

"Tell me what?" he asked.

"I'm thinking about taking the job as the town investigator," I said slowly.

Melvin jumped in the air and when he landed, I thought his feet would punch a hole in the bottom of the airboat. "Yes! Yes! That's the best news I've heard all year!"

His reaction made me feel good, and I couldn't help but grin. "Well, thanks, Melv."

"No, thank *you!*"

"Can you two stop ass-grabbing and someone hand me a pair of gloves?" Susan asked good-naturedly. I began digging in the crime scene box and she looked at Melvin. "You screamed so loud you nearly woke up our victim."

"Hell, I think I wet my pants," he said.

We all laughed, but it wasn't for long. We knew we had a killer on the loose and we had to stop him, but we also knew our work was cut out for us. Out in the swamps, there were no video cameras and rarely any witnesses. This would not be an easy case to solve.

CHAPTER 5

8:00 a.m., Tuesday, September 27
Town Hall, Mechant Loup, Louisiana

"I, Clint Wolf, do solemnly swear that I will support the Constitution and laws of the United States of America and the Constitution and laws of the State of Louisiana, and that I will faithfully and impartially discharge and perform all the duties incumbent upon me as the Chief of Detectives for the Town of Mechant Loup according to the best of my abilities and understanding, so help me God."

It was a surreal moment for me as I turned and looked out over the small group of people standing in the mayor's office to watch my swearing-in ceremony. I never thought I'd wear a badge again. I glanced down at the shield in my hand and grinned. When I looked up again, my eyes locked with Susan's and she winked.

"I am honored to present to you our first ever Chief of Detectives," Mayor Pauline Cain said to the few townspeople, government employees, and police officers, all of whom began clapping.

I wasn't sure how I would be accepted by the town, because they all knew what I'd done, but Susan had assured me they were all behind me. While I didn't care what people thought of me, I wouldn't be an effective investigator if the township despised me.

"We've got refreshments in the back," Mayor Cain said, tucking a lock of jet black hair behind her ear. "Please join us for—"

"I'm sorry, Mayor," I said, giving a sharp bow of my head. "I appreciate the gesture, but I've actually got work to do. You hired me on a busy day."

Pauline smiled warmly, and I saw her eyes cloud as she remembered how tirelessly I'd worked on her husband's case. It had been my first homicide investigation as Chief of the Mechant Loup Police Department, and it had been a hell of a case. It had caused a lot of pain and suffering for the town, especially for Pauline, who had suffered more than anyone should be allowed to suffer, having lost a son and then a husband.

She nodded her understanding. "I'll make a plate for you and send it home with Susan."

After thanking everyone who had shown up for the ceremony, I shifted the Blackhawk Serpa holster on my belt, hitched my khaki slacks a little higher on my hip, and then headed for the door.

I stepped out into the bright morning sunlight and paused at the top of the concrete steps. My head was spinning a little by how fast things had progressed. Susan had called the mayor as soon as we'd arrived at the boat launch with the victim's body last night, and Pauline had quickly gone about arranging the ceremony.

"She wants to get it done as soon as possible," Susan had joked, "before you change your mind."

I assured her I wouldn't change my mind. Susan was correct when she said she didn't have time for a death investigation, and most of her officers had never worked a murder case before, so I knew it would take a load off of her. Melvin could probably handle the case, but he shared the night rotations with Officer Amy Cooke. Pulling him away from his shift would cause Susan to be shorthanded, as there were only two other officers on the department and they were busy splitting the day shift.

Susan had to train every evening for her upcoming fight. Each time she missed a training session, it was padding her opponent's advantage. She'd assured me this would be her last fight, because she wanted to get married and focus on starting a family. While it thrilled her mom to no end and made me happy, as well, I couldn't see past this fight.

Ivanov was dangerous already, but the woman's fulltime job was fighting, while Susan's fulltime job was being a police chief. We had stayed out until ten last night interviewing the three boys who found the body, so she'd missed yet another training session. Her coach was pissed and he was starting to talk about cancelling the fight, which didn't set well with Susan and she'd threatened to fire him.

I tried to take solace in the fact that Susan was the best fighter I'd ever seen, and I assured myself she'd be fine. It was just that things had changed once I fell in love with her. I suddenly didn't like seeing her getting punched or kicked in the face; and the prospect of her getting seriously injured scared the crap out of me.

I shook my head to clear it. While I was taking this position to give Susan more time to train for her fight, truth be told, I was tickled stupid to be back on the job. Standing there in the gentle breeze—my black polo shirt tucked neatly into my khaki slacks and the gold shield and Beretta 9mm pistol weighing down my belt—it felt like I was back in the City of La Mort working as a homicide detective again. I'd been very fortunate back then. I'd amassed a 100% arrest and conviction rate for all the murder cases I'd investigated and, while most of my colleagues and supervisors thought it was because I was a great detective, I knew it was part luck, part drive, and a whole lot of prayers from my mom.

For a brief moment, a sense of pride washed over me and I felt useful again, a productive member of society—but then I remembered Michele and Abigail. The ceremony, the job, the memory…all of it conjured up powerful emotions and I bit back the lump in my throat. After all this time, the loss of my only child and wife hurt as much today as it did yesterday and the day before that and back when the incident first happened.

I grunted. *They say time's a healer, but that's bullshit. Nothing will ever heal this pain.*

My best medicine was staying busy, and it looked like this murder case was going to keep me plenty busy—

"Where're you heading, handsome?"

I blinked the moisture from my eyes and turned to smile down at Susan. "I'm heading to the autopsy first and then I'll canvass Dire Lane. Maybe someone saw something or heard gunshots one day. As of right now, we have no idea when our victim was killed."

"Well, I'm coming with you."

She'd said it as a statement, not a request, but I hesitated.

"What?" she asked.

"I'll only take you with me if you promise to leave early and get your training time in. I don't want you getting hurt in the cage."

She grunted. "Yes, father."

CHAPTER 6

"Sorry we're late," I said to Doctor Louise Wong when Susan and I stepped into the autopsy room that was located toward the back of the coroner's office. "We got tied up at the office for a bit."

Doctor Wong turned from the autopsy table, her eyes widening inside of her plastic face shield. Her mouth twisted into a grin. "Clint Wolf—is that you?"

I raised my hand as though to say, "Guilty," and just nodded.

"I thought you were done with police work." Her gloved hands glistened brightly from the mixture of blood and slop covering the latex, and the room smelled something awful. There was nothing quite like opening up a body that had been in the water for a few days to ruin your breakfast. "They said you were running some swamp tours or something."

"He's been bothering me to come back to work at the police department," Susan joked. "I finally gave in and talked the mayor into taking him back."

"I know better than that." Doctor Wong scoffed and turned back to her patient. "You were in here last year saying how much you missed working with him."

Susan glanced at me and mouthed, "I was."

I stepped closer to the autopsy table and watched as Doctor Wong shoved a probe into one of the bullet holes. She indicated with her head toward an x-ray film clasped to the white-light film viewer. "The six bullets showed up under x-ray, but I'm having a hard time getting to the last one."

I looked around and noticed five plastic containers lined up neatly on the nearby counter. I moved closer and looked inside. Each contained an oblong piece of lead. I scrunched my face. "Are these the projectiles?"

"Yeah," she said without looking up. "I labeled the side of the container to indicate which hole I pulled each one from."

I waved Susan over. "Look…they're shaped weird."

When Susan was beside me, I pointed out how the lead projectiles appeared stretched. "It looks like they squirted through a narrow hole on the way to the victim."

"Yeah," Susan agreed. "Like they went through one of those old Play-Doh squeeze toys."

"That might account for the reduction in power and lack of penetration, because whatever they squeezed through might've slowed them down enough that they didn't go through and through the body."

"Still thinking .38 or .380?"

"They're solid lead, so I'm guessing they might be some old .38 target rounds—remember the wad cutters from back in the day? They didn't have any copper on them at all and they would gum up the barrels in the worst way. I remember some of the old timers complaining about how they'd have to spend hours cleaning their revolvers."

Susan placed her hands on her hips and cocked her head sideways. The dimple on her left cheek dug deeper into her flesh as she smiled. "Um, excuse me, old man, but how on earth would I know about wad cutters?"

"We're the same age." I ripped a glove from the box on the counter and lifted one of the projectiles to the light. It was so damaged the lands and grooves from the rifling were indiscernible. "I don't think the lab will be able to match these bullets."

I gently placed it back in the plastic container and walked by Susan and stood to watch Doctor Wong wrestle the last projectile from the victim's back. It appeared identical to the other bullets. Once she'd placed that one in a separate container, she removed her gloves and pulled on a fresh pair.

"There were three potentially lethal wounds," she said. "One of the bullets perforated his heart—it's the one that actually killed him—another went through the right side of the liver and the third collapsed his left lung. Had he not been shot in the heart and had he received immediate medical attention, he might have survived the liver and lung shots, but since you didn't find him for several days, he would've died from any of these three wounds."

We stood by and waited while Doctor Wong gingerly scraped the underneath of the victim's fingernails. Once she was done, I retrieved my cadaver fingerprint kit and we set about trying to recover his fingerprints. Once we'd gotten decent sets from both hands, we set the prints to dry in the back of my new Tahoe and then returned to wrap things up with the coroner.

Doctor Wong said she would run a full toxicology report and she'd get us the results as soon as they came in. She handed us the clothes she'd removed from the body and we placed them in paper bags until we could get them to the office for air drying.

"No wallet or identification?" I asked.

Wong shook her head. "Nothing. He doesn't have a tattoo or any obvious scars. Of course, the rate of decomposition prevents us from seeing any subtle scarring."

I sighed and glanced down at my notes. "So, what we do know is he's a white male, about five-seven, has thinning white hair, was somewhere north of two hundred pounds before he ended up in the canal, and he's deadly allergic to lead."

Susan shot a thumb over her shoulder toward the exit. "Once we run his prints, we'll know if he's got a criminal record. If not…" She let her voice trail off, because we both knew how difficult it would be to identify him if his prints weren't on file and if no one had reported him missing.

I pointed to the belt that the doctor had placed on the table and turned to Susan. "That buckle"—it was an American flag in full color with the black shadow of a bear in the foreground—"is unique. If the prints don't turn up anything, we can get this out to the media. Someone might recognize it."

She nodded her agreement and I rolled it up to place it inside a bag. As I did so, I noticed an inscription on the back of the buckle. I scowled and turned it so Susan could see. "What do you think?"

"F.U.," she read slowly and then shook her head. "Right back at you, poor little man."

CHAPTER 7

After leaving the coroner's office, Susan and I drove to Dire Lane and began canvassing the neighborhood, searching for anyone who might've seen or heard anything suspicious over the course of the past few days. We parked my Tahoe on the right shoulder of the street and began making our way down that side first.

"What the hell?" Susan asked when we reached the back of the street and crossed over to the left side. "Does anyone live in this neighborhood?"

There were fourteen houses on the right-hand side, which included the homes of the three boys who had located our victim, but no one answered when we knocked.

I shrugged. "I guess all the adults are at work and all the kids are in school."

While it had been a little cooler when we stepped outside this morning, once the sun wrapped its warm arms around our town, the temperature had quickly climbed into the nineties. Sweat had gathered on Susan's forehead. As for me, I could feel it leaking down the small of my back.

We strode across the concrete surface toward the opposite side of the street. Birds chirped in the trees overhead. It was a typical neighborhood in our little town—quiet and peaceful. If gunshots were to erupt at that moment, it would shatter the tranquility of the place and cause quite a stir. I said so to Susan, but she scoffed.

"What if no one's around to hear it?" she asked.

That was a good point.

The last two lots on the left side of the street were empty. Dirt had been hauled in on one of the lots and the property had been built up, but it didn't look like construction would be taking place anytime soon. We crossed the barren lots quickly and walked up the long driveway to knock on the door to the last house on the left. Nothing.

We continued working our way toward the front of the street and met with the same results. There were eight houses on that side and, just like the right side, not a single person was home.

"It would be easy to burglarize every house in this neighborhood," Susan said, walking idly to the center of the street and surveying the area.

I lagged behind, studying the last house we'd checked, which was the first house on the left side of the street and the largest in the neighborhood. There were surveillance cameras positioned at each corner of the house. It was the only house in the neighborhood with cameras. Too bad this house wasn't located along Westway Canal.

Feeling like we'd wasted the morning, and knowing I'd have to return this evening when people were home, Susan and I grabbed a quick bite of food and I dropped her off at the police department.

"Remember our agreement," I said. "You're knocking off early and going to the gym."

"Where are you heading?"

I glanced at the clock on the dash of my Tahoe. It was two-thirty. I needed to find the spot where our victim went into the water. Once I found it, I could hopefully backtrack to the crime scene. While I could take my boat up and down the canal looking for that spot, unfortunately, I was born a city boy and didn't know an awful lot about tracking.

"I need to find out where our victim went into the water," I explained, "but I'm not the man-tracker I was in my former life."

Susan was thoughtful. "Gretchen Verdin and her dog, Geronimo, are the best K-9 team in the state. Call the sheriff and ask if you can borrow her."

I'd heard of Gretchen. She was a K-9 sergeant with the Chateau Parish Sheriff's Office and she was three-quarters Chitimacha Indian. Melvin had once told me she could track a roach across the surface of the water.

"Good idea." I leaned over to kiss her and it turned into a long moment.

When she pulled away, she smiled and rubbed my face with the tips of her fingers. She then shook her head and reached over through the gap between the seats and grabbed the evidence bags. "I'll fill out the evidence sheets and have these delivered to the crime lab. Maybe the prints will turn up something."

I then watched as she dropped from the passenger seat of my Tahoe and walked toward the front entrance of the new police department building. After the old building had burned to the ground following the gun battle with the Parker brothers last year, the town council had acquired this piece of property and built the new police department. It was located along Washington Avenue in the downtown district and was a one-story building, but that one story was twelve feet off the ground. Since we lived in hurricane country, the town council saw fit to construct a building that would withstand even the most powerful of storms while also being flood-proof. If the massive concrete pillars and solid concrete walls were any indication of strength, this building wasn't going anywhere...ever.

Once Susan disappeared inside, I pulled out my phone and called Sheriff Buck Turner to request assistance from Sergeant Verdin. Turner and I had become fast friends during my short time as Mechant Loup's police chief, and he was a man of integrity.

"I thought I heard a rumor that you were back," Sheriff Turner said. "Damn glad to hear it."

I thanked him and told him we'd recovered a body from the canal. "Do you have any missing person cases in the parish? This guy's been in the water for about three days, but Susan hasn't had any missing person reports in town."

"No, we've been busy with some dope cases and a rash of burglaries in the northern side of the parish, but we haven't had anyone disappear on us yet."

He asked about the particulars of the case. Once I'd shared what we knew so far, I asked if Sergeant Gretchen Verdin could give me a hand.

"Hell, she's on duty as we speak." He paused and I heard his radio scratch. He barked some orders and then got back on the phone with me. "Where do you want her to meet you?"

"At the boat launch in town."

"She'll be there inside of twenty minutes."

I hurried home to get my boat and then made my way back to the launch. I wanted to bring Achilles, but I figured he would try to eat Gretchen's dog, so I left him running around the back yard. There were enough squirrels back there to keep him busy for years.

CHAPTER 8

Sheriff Turner was right—Sergeant Verdin was at the boat launch within twenty minutes waiting for me. She was standing near her gray Durango with Geronimo waiting patiently by her side.

"Chief, how are you?" Gretchen asked, her tanned face lighting up when she smiled. She was slender and tall and her dark eyes were warm. Her brown hair was one length, and she had it pulled back into a short ponytail. "I was so happy when the sheriff told me you were back on the job."

"Please, just call me Clint." I stopped a few feet away from Geronimo and gave him a nod. He wasn't as tall or as heavy as Achilles, but his coat was thicker and he was a saddleback with a dark mask. He looked intimidating and not at all impressed with my greeting. I turned to Gretchen, who wore tan BDU pants and a black polo shirt with a sheriff's star embroidered over her left breast. "I appreciate the help."

She smiled again. "Well, let's see if we can find his trail before you start thanking me."

While she shrugged into her backpack, I launched my boat and then waited for her and Geronimo to board. Once they were seated in front of me, I pulled away from the launch and we set out on the water. It had cooled off a little from when Susan and I had canvassed the Dire Lane neighborhood, but it was still quite warm and the wind felt good against my face. I sped up to increase the sensation and didn't slow down until we reached Westway Canal.

Gretchen lifted a hand as I entered the mouth of the canal. "How about you hug the left side of the canal on the way down?" she suggested. "I want to get a good look at the bank on this side, and then we can make our way down the other side on the way back."

I nodded and did as she asked, taking us as close to the bank as I could without going aground. I also slowed to an idle. Gretchen's face had changed. Her eyes were narrow as she focused like a laser on the foliage along the western bank of the canal. I didn't say a word, because I didn't want to interfere with her concentration. I figured she'd tell me to stop if she located something.

I was right, because when we reached the spot where Susan and I had recovered the body, she lifted her hand. Smiling, she said, "A blind tracker could find this spot. It looks like a herd of cattle plowed through here."

She was correct. Even I could see what happened at this location. Although we'd cleaned up our mess and taken away the boards, the body, and all of our gear and trash, there were deep ruts in the soft mud that told a clear story. I could even see the impression of our victim's body still pressed into the bed of the canal.

I continued idling northward, keeping to the shadows of the western bank of the canal. Moss hung eerily from the branches overhead, which forced us to duck low from time to time, and we observed an occasional alligator floating in the water nearby.

Geronimo stood at the front of the boat, testing the water and the wind with his nose, and Gretchen carefully studied the bank. After we'd traveled about five miles up the canal, she turned and motioned for me to cross to the other side. I did and began making my way back toward the south from whence we'd come.

The shadows were growing longer now and the going was a little slower. It seemed as though we had traveled three miles when Gretchen raised a hand. I pulled back on the throttle.

She pointed. "There…look at the edge of the water."

I looked, but only saw trees and wild weeds.

"Get me as close as you can," she said.

I scanned the bank and located a shallow gulley to the right of where she wanted to be. It spilled from the wooded area to the east and appeared to be some sort of drainage ditch. I aimed the bow straight for the mouth of the gulley and pushed the throttle to gain some momentum. I pulled back when we were almost on it and allowed the boat to coast forward until it ground to a halt in the soft mud. After killing the engine, we disembarked and I tied off to a tree.

"There's a snapped twig on a low-hanging oak branch ten feet that way." Gretchen pointed toward the north. "I'll work my way to it and see if I can pick up a trail."

I nodded and settled in to wait. I pulled out my phone and

checked the time. It was a little after five. Susan should be training by now, so I didn't bother calling. I wondered if Damian Conner had made it to town yet. He was an old friend of Susan's dad and had moved to Tennessee not long after Susan's dad had died. He now ran his own boxing gym. When I'd called Damian two weeks ago—without Susan's knowledge or consent—and told him who Susan was fighting, he agreed to come down and work with her. He had heard about Antonina Ivanov and knew how dangerous she was, and he told me Susan could get hurt if she wasn't prepared.

"The woman fights men and she beats them," Damian had said when I'd called. "Why do you think the MMA champion doesn't want to fight her? You need to tell Susan to back out of this one. It's too dangerous."

"She won't listen to me," I'd said.

"She's just like her dad." He'd sighed heavily and then said he wasn't letting her go into the fight ill-prepared. "Those mixed martial arts trainers don't know shit about boxing, and she needs a good boxing coach if she wants to survive this fight."

While I'd been worrying about Susan losing, he was worried about her safety. Coming from such a highly regarded trainer, it scared the crap out of me.

I didn't know how receptive Susan would be to Damian's presence in her training camp, but he'd told me to leave that part to him—

"Clint!" Gretchen called from somewhere deep in the bush. "I've got something."

CHAPTER 9

Once I reached Gretchen and Geronimo, Gretchen pointed to a drag mark in the mud that even I could see. "This is where your victim was put into the canal." She shot a thumb over her shoulder toward the east into the trees. "I found two drops of blood a few feet that way, and it's obvious the trail continues on."

I shifted the backpack on my shoulder and lifted the camera that hung from my neck. After photographing the drag mark, I followed Gretchen into the thick of the trees, documenting the indicators she located along the way. I stopped to swab the blood spots she found because I would have to send them to the lab for comparison against the known samples from our victim. Although we were certain this was our victim's blood, we could never assume anything during criminal investigations. Every assertion we made had to be backed up with facts and evidence.

Gretchen continued snaking her way forward and I remained about twenty feet behind her and Geronimo. I kept track of our direction of travel as best I could, and it seemed we were veering toward the northeast and heading straight for Dire Lane. My suspicions were confirmed when we broke through the tree line and found ourselves in the grassy fields behind the Dire Lane neighborhood.

The going was much easier now, because Geronimo had picked up a scent and was angling straight toward the back of Dire Lane. Every few yards, or so, Gretchen would stop to point out some blood drops, and then we'd continue on. We were about fifty yards from the end of the paved road when Geronimo stopped abruptly and took a seat, indicating it was the end of the trail.

The grass in which we stood was thick and at least a foot tall. Gretchen squatted low, her butt resting on her heels, and studied the ground. She scanned the area carefully and then stood and nodded. "This is where it happened." She waved me over and pointed down through the weeds, where there were several thick pools of blood. Although the weeds were mostly tall in that area, she pointed to a smattering of bent blades. "This is where the body came to rest. It's hard to see because it's so dry out here, but a car was here a few days ago."

I followed Gretchen as she began tracking the faint tire tracks eastward until she arrived at the paved road. She straightened and looked left and right, and then turned to me. "This is where it ends."

I pointed toward the grassy path from which we'd just come, where the pools of blood had been located. "Someone killed him down there and then dragged his body all the way to the canal?"

Gretchen nodded. "That's what it looks like."

I sighed. At least I knew that much and it was now more important than ever to canvass this neighborhood. My only fear was that the murder had happened during the day when no one was home.

Gretchen and I made the long hike back to my boat and we returned to the launch. After I thanked her profusely, she left and I hitched up my boat and drove home.

It was dark when I arrived and I could hear Achilles barking as I backed the boat trailer under the carport. He always barked the same when he saw my truck or Susan's marked police Tahoe. It wasn't the deep, threatening bark he sounded when he saw a stranger or a cat. Instead, it was a yelping sound that seemed to suggest he was begging us to give him some attention.

I walked over and opened the gate to let him out of the back yard. He rushed through the opening and sat patiently, waiting for me to rub his ears. I didn't make him beg.

"What's up, big man?" I asked in the goofy voice I used while addressing him in private. "Did you miss me? Huh? Did you?"

He licked my hands with his long tongue and then bounded toward the shell road that separated our house from the gym we had built for Susan. I used it on occasion, but very rarely. There were three vehicles parked in the grass in front of the gym and I recognized two of them. The first was Susan's coach. He'd been with her from the beginning of her career and was a nice enough fellow, but Damian's words had caused me to begin doubting the crusty old fellow.

The second car belonged to Takecia Gayle, who was one of

Susan's dayshift officers and her training partner. Takecia's parents, both of them Jamaican nationals, had migrated legally to the United States over fifty years ago. About to turn twenty-four, this was the only country Takecia had ever called home and she was a proud American. As a teenager, she became an expert in judo and won the gold at the Pan American Games. She had been expected to be the first American in her weight class to take the gold in judo at the Summer Olympics, but a training injury crushed those dreams. She later went on to college, where she studied criminal justice, and eventually became a police officer. How she found her way down to our obscure town, I'll never know, but I was glad Susan had her as a training partner and an officer.

I strode across the shell driveway and stopped to study the third vehicle. It was an old Ford pickup truck, single cab, four-by-four, and it was dirty. Achilles had stopped to study it, too, and decided to pee on the rear driver's side tire. When I saw the license plate, I knew exactly to whom the truck belonged.

"Stay here, big boy," I said to Achilles, and pushed my way through the entrance and into the bright lights of the gym. There was a twelve-by-twelve boxing ring in one corner and a cage in the opposite corner, with various types of punching bags hanging from large chains scattered about the expansive room.

Sweat poured down Susan's face as she sat at the center of the boxing ring looking up at Damian Conner. Susan's coach was standing in one corner with his arms folded across his chest. I couldn't hear what Damian was saying, but Susan's coach spun and rushed toward the ropes. As he ducked through them and slipped out the ring, he hollered over his shoulder, "You'll be sorry you ever agreed to this!"

He brushed past me and I almost grabbed him by the throat and told him not to raise his voice at Susan, but I figured it was her fight and she was more than capable of handling her own affairs.

"The way a man reacts to constructive criticism says a lot about him," Damian was explaining when I leaned against the raised floor of the ring. "He couldn't even defend his method and his only answer was that I was old and washed up. Trust me, Lil' Suzy, you're better off without him."

Susan sighed and wiped a stream of sweat from her face. "I know you're right, but he got me to where I am today."

"No, good genes is what got you here," Damian said. "Any halfwit trainer can take you and make his program look good. But this girl you're fighting, she's not to be taken lightly. She's got lightning in one hand and a wrecking ball in the other."

"He's right," Takecia said in her Jamaican accent. Although she'd been raised here her whole life and her English was exceptional—even better than most Cajuns I'd encountered—she'd picked up the accent from her parents. "She is a dangerous woman. You cannot be too careful in your preparation and training."

Susan nodded and it was only then that she noticed me leaning against the ring. "Hey, Clint, look who's here," she said, shoving her thumb up in Damian's direction. "He heard about my upcoming fight and he wants to train me."

Time to 'fess up and take my beating, I thought. "Yeah, I can't imagine how he found out about it."

Susan's eyes narrowed. "Did you call him?"

"Guilty as charged."

Susan rolled smoothly to her feet and approached the ropes. She leaned through them and kissed me on the lips. "Thank you."

Damian grunted. "If you two start with that touchy-feely shit, I'm outta here."

Susan laughed and told me she had to get back to training. "Uncle D wants to work me on the mitts for a bit to evaluate where I'm at."

I nodded and told her I was cleaning up and then heading back out. "I want to canvass the Dire Lane neighborhood while people are home and before it gets too late."

"Okay." She pouted playfully, and I knew she wanted to go with me. "Have fun, Chief of Detectives."

I smiled, already feeling as though my life had real purpose again. "I will."

CHAPTER 10

It was a little after seven o'clock when I began working my way down Dire Lane—starting on the right side as we had earlier and then working my way back up the left side—and it was nearly nine when I approached the last house. Of the fourteen houses on the right, seven were occupied by young couples with no children, three were occupied by couples with one child, and the remaining four were occupied by couples with two or more children. Of the seven houses I'd already visited on the left, three were occupied by couples with two or more children, and the remaining four were occupied by couples who didn't have any children or whose children were grown. The couples with whom I'd already spoken ranged in age from early twenties to late forties, and the children living with them ranged in age from toddlers to high school seniors.

I parked my Tahoe in front of the first house on the left down Dire Lane—the name on the mailbox told me it was the Pellegrin residence—and stepped out into the warm night air. This was the house with the security cameras and I wanted very much to view the footage, but it was late and I wondered if they would allow me to do so.

I wondered when fall would actually fall as I strode up the driveway and smashed the doorbell on the side door. An elderly man answered and I imagined that he was the grandfather of the neighborhood. He was certainly the oldest person I'd encountered down the street.

After apologizing for bothering him so late into the evening, I introduced myself. "I'm investigating a homicide and was wondering if you might be able to help me."

The man, who wore long-sleeved maroon pajamas, rubbed his bare head and looked over his shoulder. "My wife is in bed…" When he turned back to me, his brow furrowed. "Did you say *homicide*?"

"Yes, sir. A man was killed at the end of the street."

He stepped back to allow me through. "We can talk in the den. I can't disturb the missus. She has work in the morning."

I followed him through his house and he pointed to a thick leather sofa. "Please, have a seat."

He settled into a recliner and asked me what he could do to help.

After asking if he'd seen anything suspicious over the past few days and him saying he hadn't, I asked if his cameras were active.

"They are." He rocked back and forth in his chair. "After we had a series of break-ins down the street a few years back, I installed cameras at every corner of the house. Fortunately, we've never had to use them."

"Would it be possible for me to get a copy of the footage for the past few days? Maybe going back to the beginning of last week?"

He nodded thoughtfully. "I can get it to you, but it would require me to make some noise in the bedroom and—"

"Oh, no, it can wait," I said, interrupting him. "I certainly don't want to risk disturbing your wife's sleep."

"She's a school teacher, so she gets up a little earlier than I do."

"It seems everyone down this street works. We canvassed the neighborhood earlier, but not a soul was home. I thought the Rapture had happened and we'd been left behind." I snickered at my own joke, but the man didn't crack a smile. Realizing it was probably best not to joke about the Rapture, I changed the subject quickly. "What time can I come by to pick up the footage?"

"I leave for work at eight, so you can come by any time before that. I'll have it ready for you." He pulled some reading glasses from a dinner tray beside his recliner and plopped them on his nose. Picking up a TV Guide, he scribbled some information on an inside page. "Everything for the past week, is that right?"

"Yes, sir. Most importantly, the footage from the cameras facing the street."

He nodded as he made his notes and then set the TV Guide back on the tray. "Okay, young man, I'll have that ready for you."

I thanked him and left. Before driving home, I decided to drive toward the back of the street to the location in the grass where our victim had been shot. I stepped out of my truck and stood looking around, listening. The sounds of crickets and frogs singing filled the stuffy air, but they were nearly drowned out by the buzzing of mosquito wings in my ears. Somewhere in the distance a coyote howled.

"Who are you and why would someone want to kill you?" I asked out loud. After calling the local sheriff offices and police departments earlier to find out if they were investigating a missing person case matching our victim's description, we had sent a teletype message through the National Crime Information Center (NCIC) computer to every law enforcement agency in the country. I pulled out my cell phone and called Marsha, who was the nighttime dispatcher. "Hey, did we receive a response from anyone on the missing person teletype?"

"Not yet," she said. "It's been quiet tonight, so I've been searching online for any news articles about missing people. There're a lot, but none matching your victim."

I was about to hang up when she stopped me.

"Oh, and there's a message for you from the day shift." I heard her shuffling about. She cleared her throat when she came back on the line. "Okay, someone from the crime lab's fingerprint department called. Who on earth wrote this message? I can't read this handwriting! Let's see…ah, it looks like it says the fingerprints were negative."

"Damn." I thanked her and put away my phone. So, our victim had never been arrested. That was good for him, but bad for me.

It was time to turn in for the night. Maybe the surveillance footage might offer some clues. I certainly hoped so. I didn't want my first case back to become a cold case.

CHAPTER 11

Wednesday, September 28

Susan and I were up early and I decided to join her and Achilles for a jog. It was about seventy degrees when we stepped outside at five-thirty in the morning, but it didn't take long for us to start sweating. We jogged down Paradise Place and didn't stop until we reached the plantation home that we'd turned into a battered women's shelter. The road was made of gravel and it felt as though we were running in sand. Susan didn't seem bothered by the degree of difficulty it presented, but I was winded and my shins ached.

"I can't wait until we can start housing women here," Susan said, stopping to admire the product of our labor. It had taken us about a year to get the place ready and we were set to open in a couple of weeks, just in time for Domestic Violence Awareness Month. "Thank you so much, Clint. I've wanted to do this forever."

I only nodded, as I leaned forward and placed my palms on my knees, trying to catch my breath. Achilles plopped down in the shade of the nearby sugarcane, which lined both sides of the road and stretched as far as the eye could see. We owned the property on which the cane grew, but had continued honoring the lease to the farmer who had worked the land for years. I certainly didn't know how to farm the land and I didn't want it to go to waste, so it was a no-brainer. Not to mention I supported all the local farmers and fishermen in every way that I could.

"Ready to run back?" Susan asked, not even winded. "Or would you rather walk?"

I took a deep breath and straightened. "I don't even know why I agreed to do this. I'm not training for anything."

"You did it because you love me and you want to watch the sunrise with me." She kissed my cheek and bolted away, her muscular legs moving effortlessly as she raced toward the front of the street.

Achilles yelped as though to say "Wait for me!"—and then twisted violently in the air, hurrying to catch up to Susan. I sighed and leaned into a steady jog, not caring that I would come in last place. I knew better than to race with either of them.

When I finally reached the house, Susan was already sitting on the backyard swing with Achilles and they were watching the orange glow forming to the east. I sat beside her and she leaned her head against my shoulder. "Thanks for calling Uncle D," she said softly. "The person I'd want training me the most would be my dad, but since he can't be here, I'm so happy Uncle D is."

I nodded idly, wondering about something she'd said Sunday night.

She noticed I was quiet and pulled away to look up at me. "What's up?"

Her movement caused the swing to sway and Achilles sat up and jumped off. He walked to the giant water bowl we kept outside for him and lapped up more of the water. After he'd had his fill, he placed both front paws in the bowl and began splashing the water around.

I laughed at Achilles, but that didn't distract Susan. "Don't ignore me," she said. "I can tell something's on your mind."

"Did you mean what you said Sunday, or was it the sex talking?"

"About having kids?"

I nodded.

"Yes, I meant every word. I'm going to take a leave of absence from work to have children." Her dark eyes searched mine. "You believe me, don't you?"

"What about fighting?"

"This'll be my last one."

"Come on, Sue, I know how much fighting means to you."

"It used to be the most important thing in my life...until you came along." She leaned her head back on my shoulder. "Now, all I want to do is start a family with you."

"Did you tell your mom this is your last fight?" I asked.

"I did."

"Damn, you're serious."

"I am."

I listened to the chain squeak above us as we gently rocked back and forth. The sun was slowly peeking over the distant treetops and birds began singing in the trees overhead. I smiled, wanting to remain in this moment forever. There's nothing like sitting on a swing with the woman you love watching the sun come up while your best friend is fighting with his water bowl—

I suddenly jumped to my feet. "What time is it?"

She glanced at her watch. "Six fifty-four…why?"

"I have to be on Dire Lane before eight." I raced for the door to take a quick shower. "I need to hurry."

"You're not going without me," she said, matching me step for step.

CHAPTER 12

I pulled into Mr. Pellegrin's driveway with five minutes to spare. He was already walking to his car carrying a light jacket and a newspaper when we arrived.

"I didn't think you would make it," he said, placing his jacket on the front seat of his old car. "I thought you might have been called away to something more pressing."

I introduced him to Susan and he nodded. "I remember you, Chief. You did a presentation for my wife's class last year. Saw your picture in the paper with them."

"Ah, I remember," Susan said. "Fine group of kids, that bunch."

They chitchatted for a few seconds and then he fished a palm-sized external flash drive out of his shirt pocket and handed it to me. "This is everything you requested."

I thanked him and he nodded.

"If you'll excuse me now, I have to leave before I'm late for work." He turned and shuffled back to his car.

Susan and I got in my Tahoe and I drove to the police department, where I parked under the building. We then walked up the thick concrete steps at the front of the building and entered the lobby. Lindsey, who was the daytime dispatcher, waved and buzzed us through the left-side entrance. We entered a hallway and passed the women's bathroom, which was on the right, and Susan pointed to the second door on the left. "This is your office."

I glanced toward the third and last door to the left, which was her office, and smiled. "I like that you put me next-door to you."

"I figure if you're going to work here, I might as well see as much of you as possible."

My office was already furnished. There was a desk, two tall metal filing cabinets, a large wooden bookcase, and two visitors' chairs. I walked around my desk and took a seat behind the computer. After turning it on, I plugged the wire for the external hard drive into the USB port.

Susan had dragged one of the visitors' chairs around the desk and plopped in it beside me. Once the computer fired to life and I'd opened the file folder on the hard drive, I grunted. There were three different camera angles covering twenty-four hours of five days. "This'll take forever."

"Yep." Susan grabbed a notepad and ink pen and nodded her head. "Let's do it."

I picked the angle that focused on the front of the street, because I could see any vehicles coming or going and would be able to determine their direction of travel once getting onto Main Street. We began at the Monday morning mark and started watching footage. At first, it was difficult to determine what was suspicious or out of the ordinary because we didn't know which cars were supposed to be coming and going, but after watching three days of video, we began to recognize a pattern.

"The same cars leave every morning and return every evening," Susan noted. "And they almost all leave at the same time."

I nodded. Other than the mail truck or an occasional delivery van, there was no traffic on the street between nine in the morning, when the last car left, and two-thirty in the afternoon, when the first bus arrived to drop off school kids. Afterward, between four and six, the same cars that had left in the morning began returning.

It was lunchtime before we made it to Thursday's film, so we stopped and walked down the street to grab a hamburger. On the walk back to the office, we were approached by a few passersby who needed to speak with the chief of police about various issues, and I enjoyed watching Susan solve their problems. She was a natural, and everyone loved her.

"You're really good at this," I said. "I can't imagine you giving it up."

Susan brushed at a lock of hair that had escaped the ponytail on the right side. "Kids are more important than some job."

"Can't you do both?"

She was thoughtful, but didn't say anything as we stepped back into the police department. Takecia was standing over Lindsey waiting for a computer printout. She waved through the bulletproof glass that separated the lobby from the dispatcher's station.

"Same time tonight, Chief?" she asked, grinning wide to expose a row of bright teeth. "I get to choke you out again, yeah?"

"Same time," Susan said, pushing through the entrance and into the hallway. When we were seated back at my desk, she explained how they had drilled rear-naked choke escapes last night. "Takecia's got a death grip on her. She's awesome at submissions."

Not wanting to dwell on the mental image of my future wife being choked out, I pulled up the Thursday video and hit the *play* button. We ran it in fast motion forward, just as we had with the other videos, and we'd only stop when we saw something that appeared unfamiliar—like the blue truck that had turned down the street at eight o'clock in the morning. It was only the second time we'd seen that truck. The first time was on Wednesday at two-thirtyish. It had turned down the street behind one of the buses, but it left shortly thereafter.

As the minutes ticked by on the video, the truck didn't reappear. Thinking we were on to something, we sped the video up a little and watched closely. We were both leaning forward, our heads almost touching, when the blue truck reappeared about an hour later.

"Can you make out a license plate?" I asked, pausing the film and zooming the image.

"No, it's too blurry."

I sighed and continued playing the video. When we reached midnight, I clicked on the Friday file and began playing that one next.

"We'd better find something soon," Susan said. "We're running out of days."

She was right. If we didn't find anything on Friday or Saturday, that meant we had either gone too fast through the videos or our victim had gotten a ride to the neighborhood with one of the residents. I began to voice the idea when Susan stopped me.

"Wait—back up. It's the blue truck again."

I hit the *pause* button on the video and began playing it backward. We had rushed through the dark hours and nothing appeared out of the ordinary. When I rewound the film to eight-thirty-seven in the morning, the blue truck came into view. Susan stabbed at the screen with her finger. "It's the same truck from Wednesday and Thursday."

I zoomed in on the image and we could clearly see it was a small Nissan King Cab with a camper shell over the bed. It was old, at least twenty years. After saving a screen capture of it, I continued playing the video in forward motion and we watched closely, waiting for it to reappear. It never did.

I accessed the video files from Saturday through Monday, but we never saw the truck again.

"We need to account for that truck." I drummed my fingers on the desk. "It either belongs to a resident or it's our victim's truck."

"If that was our victim, where's the truck?"

I didn't have an answer, so I set about printing copies of the screenshot of the truck. I glanced at the digital clock at the bottom corner of my computer screen. It was almost five. We had spent all day looking at video surveillance footage. While it wasn't a complete waste, it certainly didn't feel like a productive day—especially since a killer was still walking around free.

I gathered up the pictures and stood. Susan stood with me and we both turned when we heard boots pounding outside the door. It was Melvin.

"Any progress?" he asked.

"Not much." I handed him a couple of the pictures. "Have you ever seen this truck around town?"

He held the top picture close to his face and studied it for a long moment. Finally he shook his head. "It doesn't look familiar."

"Give Amy a copy," Susan said, "and y'all keep an eye out for it. There's a good chance it belonged to our victim."

When Melvin walked off, Susan told me she was heading to the gym and I followed her to the parking lot. For me, it was back to Dire Lane to see if anyone recognized the blue truck.

CHAPTER 13

Thursday, September 29

Susan and Achilles were still out running when I left home this morning, but I needed to get to the office and start making phone calls.

I'd spoken to most of the neighbors on Dire Lane last night and handed out a dozen pictures of the truck, but no one remembered seeing it down their street. I had met with Mr. Pellegrin last and asked if he could keep feeding me footage from his surveillance camera, just in case the truck left the neighborhood when no one was looking. He said he was happy to oblige. I replaced his hard drive with one comparable to what he had given me, and also gave him an additional hard drive on which to store subsequent footage.

Lindsey buzzed me through the door and I stepped into the dispatcher's station. Her door was directly across the hall from my office, which would most likely prove convenient.

"Hey, um—do I still call you chief?" she asked, setting aside a paperback novel she was reading.

"Just call me Clint." I walked to the pigeonhole they'd set up for me and looked inside. There was a message from the ballistics examiner at the crime lab. I snatched it up and stopped by Lindsey's desk. "I'm guessing there's been no response from our teletype message about missing persons?"

She frowned. "Not yet. I'll let you know as soon as I hear something, though."

I thanked her and walked to my office. I called the firearms examiner, whose name was Vanessa, and told her I was returning her call.

"Detective Wolf, these projectiles you submitted are definitely a first," she said. "While we can't use the striation marks from the rifling, I've been able to determine that all six bullets were fired from the same weapon."

"How so?" I asked. "They looked too deformed for comparative analysis."

"This was really an intriguing study," she said. "The deformities are identical and, at first, I couldn't figure out what caused them. But, after studying them carefully, I realized they were fired from a revolver with a misaligned cylinder. When the cartridge is fired, the bullet is forced through the narrow opening like—"

"One of those Play-Doh squeeze toys," I said, interrupting her to finish her sentence.

"Yeah...how'd you know?" she asked, sounding a little bewildered.

"Chief Susan Wilson"—it rolled off my tongue awkwardly, as I was not used to calling Susan by her official title—"described them that way out at the scene."

"Well, that's an accurate description. So, you're looking for a .38 caliber revolver with a misaligned cylinder."

I thanked her and hung up the phone. The picture of the blue truck was on my desk and I studied it. It was last seen at almost nine on Friday. Based on what we'd seen, no one from the neighborhood would've been around to hear the gunshots, but, if that were true, there'd also be no one around to fire the shots.

I turned to my computer and checked our electronic database of complaints from Friday morning to see if anyone had reported hearing gunshots. Nothing. Perhaps the killer was a passenger in the vehicle?

Desperate, I called Ali Bridges, who used to be Chloe Rushing's intern at the news station and who now worked as a reporter for the *Mechant Voice*, a new newspaper that had opened up in town. They covered local news and events, as well as things that happened in the parish and around the state.

"Ali Bridges of *Mechant Voice*," called her sweet voice over the phone. "How may I help you?"

"It's Clint Wolf at the police department."

"Chief Wolf! I'm glad you called." She sounded excited to hear from me, which I thought was odd. "I heard you were back. I want to do a story on you."

My shoulders slumped. I hated being interviewed for personal stories. I didn't mind providing information on cases, but I didn't like talking about myself. Instead of addressing it, I decided to just pretend she hadn't even said it. "So, I'm sure you heard we recovered a body from Westway Canal Monday evening."

"I did," Ali said. "We ran a little piece from the press release Chief Wilson sent out."

I hadn't seen it, but I didn't read the newspaper much anyway. "Well, we might have a break in the case, but I need your help to disseminate some information."

"Sure, I'm happy to help."

I explained about the truck and asked if she could run an ad asking anyone who might've seen the truck to call the office. "I'll drop off a picture of the truck in a minute, if that's good with you."

"It's perfect—I can interview you for the story while you're here."

I groaned out loud, but then instantly felt bad about it. "Sure, Ali. No problem."

I drove to the paper to drop off a picture of the truck, and I spent thirty minutes answering Ali's questions. She recorded me and I didn't like it one bit, but I didn't object. After we were done, she said, "I've already spoken to my editor and the ad about the truck will go out this afternoon. The article about your return to the police force will be in tomorrow's paper."

I made a mental note to avoid tomorrow's paper and thanked her for running the ad on such short notice. I then returned to the office to start cold-calling sheriffs' departments and police departments around the state. I had a thick book that listed every law enforcement agency in Louisiana, and I was determined to call each of them.

I worked until lunch on the calls, but I kept coming up dry. Only two of the fifty agencies I called so far had active missing person cases, but neither of the victims were white male subjects.

"Hey, do you want to grab some lunch with me?" Susan asked, sticking her head in my office.

I pushed away from my desk and sighed heavily. "It's been three days and I'm no closer to identifying this guy than we were when we found him face-up in the mud."

She stepped fully into my office and leaned her back against the door frame. "Something'll give. It always does."

"I'm not so sure about this one. If the killer never says a word to anyone and we never identify our victim, this could go unsolved." I turned my computer monitor to show her what I'd been researching while on the phone. "I'm thinking about finding someone to reconstruct his face. There's a team of forensic artists in Baton Rouge who do this kind of thing. Maybe it would help."

She smiled. "You're the chief of detectives. It's your call."

I nodded and got up to join her.

CHAPTER 14

Susan and I strode down the stairs and walked out onto the sidewalk. It was another beautiful day. The sun was shining and people were bustling about on the sidewalks. There were dozens of shops and a few restaurants along Washington Avenue, and you would swear no one was working today with the amount of people milling about.

We headed for one of the burger dives down the street and had almost reached it when I heard a little boy begging his mom for a hamburger and a chocolate shake. I didn't blame him. The aroma of fried beef and grilled onions was so thick in the air it almost slowed us down.

I glanced toward the mom and kid and saw that the young lady wore a short brown sundress and sandals. The little boy—who couldn't have been more than four—wore jean shorts and a T-shirt with stains on the front. I gritted my teeth when I saw the inside of the woman's left arm.

"You know we can't afford to eat out, Sammy," the young woman said, tugging on his arm. Her dirty blonde hair looked like it needed a trim and the polish on her fingernails was chipped. "Now, come on. We have to get to the electric company before they shut off our power."

She brushed by us without even looking up, but I could see the sadness in her eyes and a mark on her cheek that was mostly covered by makeup.

"Ma'am," I called when she walked by. "Excuse me, miss…"

She hesitated and then turned her head. Her shoulders fell when she saw Susan's uniform and my badge and gun. "Yes? Did I do something wrong?"

"Not at all, ma'am. I just want to say hello to your boy." I walked over and squatted to my knees, extending my hand to little Sammy. "How are you, little man?"

He wrapped an arm around his mom's bare knee and hid his face behind her dress. He didn't say anything, but peeked around her with a curious glint in his eye.

"You know I was your age once?" I asked. "What are you— twenty years old?"

That brought a giggle from the boy. He shoved out his hand, holding up four fingers. "I'm this many," he said. "My birthday's in too many days and I'm gonna be six."

"Five," his mom corrected.

I stood and pulled my wallet from my back pocket. "I'd like to buy you and Sammy lunch."

The young lady scowled. "Um…why?"

"Because I know how it feels to crave a hamburger." I examined the contents of my wallet. I had four twenties, five tens, six fives, and four ones. I dug it all out and shoved it toward the lady. "Here, lunch is on me."

"That's…that's way too much," she said slowly. "I can't accept this."

"Either you take it, or I drop it on the ground."

That brought a flash of a smile. Her green eyes glistened for a brief moment and then the light faded.

"Are you sure?" she asked, her voice timid.

"Absolutely." I reached forward and placed the money directly in her hand. "Enjoy your lunch."

As Susan and I turned to walk inside the restaurant, which was called Bad Loup Burgers, I heard the little boy say, "Mommy, that was a nice policeman."

"Yes, honey, it sure was."

"Did you see the bruises on her arm and face?" I asked Susan when we sidled up to the bar.

"I did. I almost asked her about it, but there were too many people on the streets."

I nodded and glanced toward the entrance to the restaurant, but she was already gone.

We ordered our food and took a seat at a back corner table to wait. Before our food arrived, the screen door opened and the young woman and Sammy walked into the place. I figured she'd gone to pay her electric bill. Sammy was smiling wide and nearly jumping for joy. They sat at one of the booths and the woman glanced over to where we were. She smiled warmly and mouthed the words, "Thank you."

Susan stood abruptly. "I'm going talk to her."

I watched as the lady I wanted to marry strode across the dimly lit place and stopped near the woman's table. They spoke briefly and Susan pulled a card from her shirt pocket. She scribbled something on the back of the card—I knew it was her cell number—and handed it to her. The woman smiled and nodded her head. She tucked the card into her bra when Susan walked away, and then she leaned into Sammy and pointed to the menu.

"What'd you tell her?" I asked.

"I told her we were opening up a shelter for battered women and their children," she said. "I asked that she spread the word around in case any of her friends were being abused by their husbands or boyfriends."

It made my heart happy to see the smile on little Sammy's face, but I was also sad as I wondered what kind of life they lived. It was possible the bruises were the result of hard work, but I had my doubts. When my mom would work in her garden years ago, she'd always end up with bruises up and down her arms and legs, but they didn't look like fingertips and she never got one on her cheek.

Susan reached across the table and squeezed my hand. "That was nice of you."

Not wanting to dwell on it, I just shrugged and looked up in time to see the waitress approaching with a tray of burgers, fries, and chocolate milkshakes.

We devoured our food and were back at the office within the hour. Susan had to answer a call and I went back to contacting police departments and sheriffs' offices. There were over three hundred law enforcement agencies in Louisiana and I contacted every one of them. No one had a missing person that matched our victim's description.

My ear aching from being pressed up against a phone all day, I left the office and drove home. Susan was in the gym with Takecia and Damian. Achilles was sitting patiently by the door waiting for them to exit. I rubbed his ears on the way through the door.

"Did they lock you out, big man?" He whined—which sounded a lot like affirmation—and I slipped inside, promising to play with him when I was done.

Damian and Susan were moving in unison around the ring. Damian was holding punch mitts and Susan was attacking fiercely when he called out combinations. He spoke in boxing code, the words rolling rapidly off his tongue, and his hands moved like pistons.

Susan's eyes were narrow slits as she moved gracefully around the ring, stalking Damian like an angry tiger. When she fired off her punches, they were explosive and smacked violently against the mitts, echoing loudly throughout the gym.

"Your girl is good," Takecia said when I moved beside her and leaned against the raised boxing ring. "If she is careful, she will win."

While Takecia specialized in judo, she had a varied skill set and had enjoyed a successful career as a cage fighter. Her opinion counted and it made me feel better. I couldn't stand the thought of Susan losing or—worse—getting hurt.

After about thirty minutes of working the mitts, the buzzer sounded to end fifteen rounds of work. Susan spat her mouthpiece from her mouth and shoved a gloved hand toward Damian. "*That's* what's been missing from my training!"

Damian nodded his head and his face twisted into a confident scowl. "You'll be ready in four weeks." He waved Susan over and began stripping the boxing gloves off of her hands. "You punch like your dad. By the end of the month, you'll be blocking like me. It's the best combination you could ask for and, if you play it safe, you could win this thing."

Susan's face glistened with sweat. She was breathing heavy, but she was smiling. "I feel great, Clint. I'm going to knock her ass out."

"Easy," Damian said. "Don't start making predictions. We'll devise a plan and you'll execute that plan. If the knockout comes, it comes. If it doesn't, that's fine, too. Our goal is to win and not take a beating. You certainly don't want to go toe-to-toe with her. We're going to exploit her weaknesses while enhancing your strengths."

"Yes, sir." Once Susan's hands were free, she picked up her gloves, and Takecia and I helped her clean up the gym. Afterward, when everyone was gone, she and I retired to the house and took a shower before dinner. When we finally sat to eat, she asked me if I'd made any headway on the case.

"Nope." I chewed idly as I watched Achilles wolf through his bowl of food. "Nothing."

"I saw the truck in the three o'clock paper," she offered, sounding hopeful. "Maybe that'll generate some tips."

I hoped she was right, but wasn't counting on it. If no one down Dire Lane saw the truck, there was little chance someone around town did. Besides, the Dire Lane neighborhood was located in the incorporated area north of the Mechant Loup Bridge and the blue truck had approached from the north, so it might've never ventured into the heart of town. We'd have a better chance of someone in Chateau Parish seeing it, but even that might be a long shot. People usually didn't notice vehicles unless someone did something to attract attention.

CHAPTER 15

6:12 a.m., Friday, September 30
Baylor Rice's residence, Mechant Loup, Louisiana

Officer Baylor Rice, who had become the newest member of the Mechant Loup Police Department earlier last year, hitched up his gun belt as he stepped out of his marked police car. He had reported to work twenty minutes ago and had barely gotten the pass-on information from Officer Amy Cooke for Thursday night when Lindsey received the call. It was from a Beth Gandy over on North Pine Street and she was in hysterics.

Before Baylor could make his way up the drive, a woman dressed in a thin nightgown rushed to him, wringing her hands and shaking her head. The words gushed from her mouth. "I...I don't know where Troy could be. He's never done anything like this. It's not like him to just up and disappear. Oh, my God, what if something bad happened to him? What if someone came into our home and took him? I see this kind of thing on TV—"

"It's okay, ma'am," Baylor said in a soothing tone. "I'm here to help you find him, okay?"

The woman nodded and began chewing on her lower lip. "Okay."

"Are you Beth Gandy?"

She nodded her head up and down.

"Okay...why don't you take a deep breath and begin by telling me how you came to notice Troy was missing?"

Beth took a deep and trembling breath and then began speaking rapidly again. "I...he missed the bus. I heard the bus pass and I realized he hadn't gotten up yet, so I went to his room. He keeps his door locked. I used to fuss him about that, but then one day about two years ago I used this little key I have to go into his room because I thought he was doing drugs. When I went in, he was…"

Beth paused and Baylor noticed that her face was burning red. He got the picture and lifted a hand. "It's okay…you don't have to say it."

She nodded and continued. "I was so embarrassed and he was even more embarrassed than I was. We didn't look at each other or speak for about a day. I've raised him alone. His dad's never been around, so it's difficult, you know, being a woman and having to talk to your son about those kinds of boy feelings and all."

Trying to be patient, Baylor nodded as she rattled on. Finally, he interjected and asked again if she could tell him how she first noticed her son was missing.

"Well, when I heard the bus pass and I hadn't heard the front door slam and he hadn't stopped to tell me good-bye, I got up and went to check on him. His door was locked and he wouldn't answer. I banged on the door really loud, but it didn't wake him up. I got really scared at that point and thought maybe he was sick." She shuddered, as the memory of the moment seemed to come back to her. "Although I swore I'd never do that again, I took my little key and opened the door and…and he was just gone. He wasn't there. Someone must've come in the house and taken him. I…I don't know what to do. I don't know what happened."

"Okay, ma'am," Baylor said in his low voice. "Show me to his room and I'll see what I can figure out."

Hugging herself, the woman led the way up the short steps and into the living room of her modest home. Baylor took in his surroundings as he followed her, scanning for dangers and any obvious signs that might explain her son's disappearance.

They walked down a long dark hallway and then Beth moved to the right side of the hall and pointed toward the opposite door. "That's his room."

Baylor had less than one year on the job, but he'd served four years in the United States Marines and he'd learned to be wary of traps and other dangers.

Not wanting to sound any alarm bells if this was indeed a trap, he motioned with his head toward the door. "Why don't you reenact what happened when you came to his room? It'll help me get a sense of things."

Beth nodded and stepped forward, providing nervous commentary as she went through the motions of unlocking the door and pushing it open. Once Baylor could see inside the room and verify that everything was clear, he followed her inside. The room was a typical boy's room. Cluttered and messy. There were empty plates with food scrapings on a small desk near the bed. Empty cups and candy wrappers littered the floor.

"Excuse the mess."

Baylor just nodded and moved around the room. There were no signs of a struggle, no forced entry on the door, and no one was hiding in the closet or under the bed. He moved to the window and pulled back the curtain. Light was starting to shine through the window as dawn began to break to the east, and he could clearly see that the window was closed, but unlocked. Upon closer inspection, he also noticed the screen had been removed and was resting in the damp grass below.

"Ma'am, has your son ever run away from home?"

A bewildered expression fell across Beth Gandy's face. "No...why would you ask such a thing?"

Baylor shot a thumb toward the window. "It looks like he left through the window and then closed it back to cover his tracks."

Beth rushed forward and looked out the window. "Are you sure?"

"I'm afraid so. How did your son get around?"

"Get around?" There was a blank expression on Beth's face as she tried to process what she was learning. "What do you mean?"

"Does he drive yet?"

"He has his permit, but he can't drive without me."

"What about a bicycle or four-wheeler or something? How does he get around the neighborhood?"

"He has a bicycle."

"What does it look like?"

"It's black and silver. It's one of those dirt bikes you can ride in the woods and all."

"Where does he keep it?" Baylor asked.

Beth turned and walked out of the room. Baylor followed her down the hallway, through the dining room, out the side door, and into the garage. Her shoulders fell when she turned the corner. She pointed to the space between her car and the garage wall. "That's where he keeps his bike, but it's...it's gone. He's gone. My boy is gone."

Baylor frowned as he watched Beth. She looked deflated. Wanting to keep her focused and talking, he asked her what time she saw Troy last.

"We had dinner at seven-thirty, or thereabouts. I took a bath afterward and Troy went to his room. I knocked on his door at nine to tell him good night. That was the last time I spoke to him."

Baylor made a note of the time frame—between nine o'clock last night and six this morning, when the call came in. "Where do you think Troy would go?" he asked.

"I...I don't know." She pulled her cell phone from a pocket in her nightgown and pressed some buttons. She put it to her ear and waited. "There's no answer. I've called a dozen times, but it just keeps ringing and ringing."

"What about his dad? Do they ever talk or visit?"

Beth waved her hand dismissively. "When Troy was younger, he wanted to have a relationship with his dad—to be normal like the other boys, you know? All we had was an address and he wrote plenty of letters, but his dad never responded. I knew that would happen, but I had to let Troy find out for himself. Otherwise, he would've blamed me for them not having a relationship."

At Baylor's request, Beth provided all the names of his aunts and uncles and grandparents.

"I've called them all, but no one has heard from him."

"What about his friends?"

"He doesn't really have any friends." She frowned. "He just goes to school and comes home. He's a momma's boy."

"Did you guys have a disagreement of any kind yesterday, or any time recently?"

Beth shook her head. "We don't ever argue. He's a good kid. He does everything I ask him to do and he never complains about it."

While all the evidence pointed to Troy leaving the house willingly, Baylor didn't feel comfortable driving away from the scene without notifying Chief Wilson. If something bad had happened to Troy Gandy, he didn't want it said later that he dropped the ball.

CHAPTER 16

"Clint, can you give Baylor Rice a hand?" Susan called from the hallway. "He's working a missing person case and he's hit a wall. It looks like the boy left of his own will, but he didn't seem to have a reason to run away. They've checked with everyone he knows and no one's heard from him."

It was a little after seven and I was sitting on the edge of our bed lacing up my boots. I stopped for a second, scowled. "A missing person? Is it possible he's our murder victim?"

She walked into the doorway of the bedroom wearing only her sports bra and panties. My jaw must've dropped, because the corner of her mouth curled up into a little grin. "No, he disappeared last night," she said. "It's some kid named Troy Gandy. He lives on North Pine."

That immediately got my attention. I shoved my holster into my beltline and rose to my feet. North Pine was located in the newly incorporated part of Mechant Loup just north of the bridge—and it was one street over from Dire Lane.

I looked up and shook my head as I stared at Susan's half naked self. "How am I supposed to leave the house with you looking like that?"

She giggled and moved forward to hug me. I pulled her firm, but also soft, body into me and we kissed for much longer than I should have. When our mouths separated, she remained in place, frozen in time. Her eyes were half closed and her lips slightly parted. If she were a cat, she would've purred.

"I love you," I said softly.

"I love you more." She shook her head to clear it. "I'll take a quick shower—a very cold one—and meet you out there. Just let me know what's going on and where to go."

I kissed her again, but briefly, and then rushed out the door. Achilles ran to the gate near the patio and yelped furiously at me as I rushed to my Tahoe. He had grown accustomed to riding in the boat with me every day when I was running swamp tours, and I think he missed me. I certainly missed him and wished I could take him to work with me, but it wasn't possible.

I quickly turned around and ran to the gate. "Hey, buddy, I'll be back," I said, rubbing the area around his big ears. "While I'm gone, make sure to keep the house safe. Okay?"

He cocked his head sideways, a confused look on his face. I could just as well have been speaking Belarusian or some other obscure language, because he had no clue what I was saying.

After a final pat on the head, I turned and rushed to my Tahoe and sped out the driveway. I called Baylor Rice on the police radio and asked him where to meet.

He radioed back and gave me the address on North Pine. It was going to be my first time working with Baylor, but Susan and Melvin had nothing but good things to say about him over the months he'd been there.

Susan had hired Baylor last year right after she'd hired Takecia Gayle. It had increased her number of officers to four and enabled her to run twelve-hour shifts, with at least one officer covering the town at all times. Melvin and Amy, her most seasoned officers, worked the night shift while Baylor and Takecia worked the day shift.

Mayor Cain had authorized overtime pay for any officer wanting to work extra duty to serve as backup during peak hours, and Baylor was always volunteering.

Twenty-four and single, Baylor was originally from a small town in North Carolina called Sylva and he had found his way to Mechant Loup after doing a four-year stint in the military. When first meeting him a few months ago, I'd asked how it was that someone from a small town in the mountains could end up in a small town in the swamps, and he'd said one of his military buddies told him about this place.

"He was from a place called Mathews and he said he used to come to Mechant Loup to fish." Baylor had frowned and stared down at his boots. "He said it was the closest he could find to Heaven on earth, and it's where he wanted to live out his days when he got out the service."

I found out later that his friend had died in a helicopter crash during a training exercise in California, and he had come to Mechant Loup to live out his friend's dream.

Baylor sounded like a young man with character, and I was glad he had found his way to our little paradise.

CHAPTER 17

I parked my Tahoe behind Baylor's marked patrol car and met him on the front concrete porch of the Gandy home. Baylor was an inch shorter than me and not as stocky, but he appeared to be fit. I leaned around him and stared through the glass door, where I saw a tearful Beth Gandy pacing back and forth in the living room, a phone pressed to the side of her head.

"What do we know so far?" I asked.

He told me it appeared Troy had snuck out the back window and left on his bicycle. "His mom's on the phone with one of his cousins who lives an hour away, but they say they haven't heard from him. None of their other relatives have heard from him."

I nodded and watched the woman, wondering if this could be connected to our victim who was still lying in the morgue unidentified. "What about his cell phone?"

"He took it with him."

"Does he have a wallet?"

Baylor nodded. "It's also missing, so it looks like he left on his own accord."

"This might be nothing more than a runaway case." I pulled my attention away from the mother and asked about the father, and Baylor told me he was absent from the boy's life.

I was mulling over our next move when the front door opened and Beth Gandy stepped out. Tears flowed from her eyes. "No one's seen him or heard from him. It's not like him to do something like this."

I introduced myself to her and asked if Troy had a computer.

She nodded.

"Do you mind if we go through it?"

She shrugged. "Sure, I guess. He doesn't like me going through his personal things, but if it'll help locate him…"

She led us to his bedroom, which was a mess, and I pointed to his laptop. "Baylor, you're closer to his age…would you like to give it a shot?"

"Sure," he said, grinning. "I'm probably a little more versed on the latest social media crave, considering the specks of silver in your hair."

I ignored him. At thirty-two years of age, I'd seen more than most people see in a lifetime, so I forgave myself for the gray hair that had begun cropping up here and there since last year.

While Baylor sat at the desk to go through Troy's computer, I began searching the bedroom. Mrs. Gandy walked away and I could hear her crying softly in the hallway. The entire floor seemed to be covered in stuff—some of it good, but most of it garbage—and I had to check every item to make sure it wasn't of evidentiary value. I had finally worked my way to Troy's closet when Susan called me.

"Hey, do you need anything?" she asked. "I'm heading that way."

"Can you contact the service provider for Troy Gandy's cell phone and see if they can ping it?"

"Sure, send me the info in a text message. I'll swing by the office and contact them. What exigent circumstances do I list as the justification?"

"'Troy Gandy disappeared suddenly and suspiciously from his bedroom a quarter of a mile from where a man was found murdered'…that should do it, right?"

She agreed and we ended the call. I got the number and service provider information from Mrs. Gandy, and then sent it in a message to Susan. Afterward, I continued searching the room, but didn't locate anything of interest. "I've got nothing," I said to Baylor. "I didn't even find his porn stash."

"I did." Baylor tilted the laptop so I could see the screen. "This is how the Post-Millennials roll, sir. The days of sneaking your dad's Playboy magazine from the bathroom cabinet are over. Every young boy's fantasy is now as close as his fingertips."

"What's this world coming to?" I grumbled, closing the closet doors. It was still early in the case, but I didn't want to take any chances. While he might've run away from home, there was a murderer at large and Troy might've run into trouble. I needed to organize a search party and we needed to start combing the neighborhood.

Since Baylor and Melvin were covering the weekend on their regular shift, I called Susan and asked if Amy and Takecia could assist with the search.

"Clint, I don't think I can ever get used to you asking me for permission to do anything. You were *my* chief, remember? You can always call out whoever you need to call out and whenever you need them."

"Well," I began. "I won't stand for you calling out any of my detectives without running it by me first."

"Yeah, all none of them, right?" She laughed and told me she'd call them to meet us on North Pine.

She didn't waste any time, because Amy arrived minutes later. Her blonde hair was pulled back in a ponytail and she wore tight jeans and a snug-fitting T-shirt. Her pistol was tucked into the paddle holster in her pants and she held a notebook in her left hand. "Where do you want me to start?" she asked, always ready to work.

"You take this side," I said, indicating with my head toward the north side of the street. "I'll take that side."

There wasn't a cloud in the sky and the day had gotten much warmer. Sweat was pouring down my face by the time I'd made it to the second house, and it didn't get any better as I progressed through the neighborhood. Like Dire Lane, there weren't many people home at that early hour on North Pine Street. Everyone was either at work or school, and those who were home hadn't seen anything.

As I neared the end of the street, I made contact with an elderly man who was plucking vegetables from tall vines situated in neat rows behind his house. After asking about Troy and finding out he knew nothing, I thought to ask how often he tended his garden.

"Every day," he said with a grunt, as though I should've already known the answer. "If you skip one day, you'll get behind. And once you get behind, there's no catching up."

"So, you were in your garden Friday morning?"

"Like I said, I'm here every day."

"Did you hear any gunshots that morning?"

The man stopped what he was doing and straightened. He squinted and glanced up at the sky, thinking. "You know what? I did."

"What time?" I asked.

"Oh, it had to be around nine in the morning. There were five or six of them, one after the other." He shrugged. "We're always hearing shots back here, so we don't get too worked up over it. But these were different."

"Different? How?"

"Most of the shots we hear are from hunting guns—rifles and shotguns. This one sounded smaller than those, like a handgun."

"Are you sure?"

"I served in the Vietnam War, son—I know what a handgun sounds like."

After asking a few more questions, I nodded and thanked him for his time. "You've been a big help."

As I walked away, I considered the timeline that was forming. The blue Nissan truck was picked up by the surveillance camera at eight-thirty-seven and the victim was most likely shot around nine o'clock. What had our victim done in those twenty-three minutes? Who had he pissed off in that short amount of a time?

I continued pondering those questions and others as I finished canvassing my side of the street. When I was done, I met with Amy in front of the Gandy home again.

"Anything?" I asked.

She frowned and shook her head. "You?"

I told her about the man who'd heard the gunshots. "Now we know a time, but nothing else."

Amy and I then met with Baylor and Takecia and we all hit the fields behind the house. There were no bike tracks and the fields were dry and rugged, but we checked them anyway. Nothing was off-limits and there were no wrong answers with this case. I was willing to try anything, as long as it increased the odds of finding Troy before something bad happened to him.

After we searched the fields behind the Gandy home, we strode to the opposite side of the street and searched the fields between Dire Lane and North Pine. We met with the same results—nothing but dried mud, thick weeds, and the occasional snake slithering around.

Takecia wiped sweat from her dark cheeks. "If this boy is having a good time with a girl right now, I will kick his ass when we find him."

I sighed as I looked up and down the street. "How can this kid just disappear into thin air?"

"Did you notice any houses with surveillance cameras?" Baylor asked.

I shook my head and turned to Amy. "You?"

"No," she said. "Not one."

My phone rang and I pulled it idly to my ear. "This is Clint."

"The cell phone company pinged Troy's phone," Susan said. "I'm sending you the GPS coordinates now, along with a map. The location is north of where you are."

I scowled as I waited for the information to arrive on my phone. We had worked our way north to the next street but hadn't seen anything. Of course, we were looking for something the size of a human—not a tiny cell phone.

When the coordinates arrived, I enlarged them on my phone and studied the map Susan had sent. There were two paved streets north of North Pine and then a third street that was longer than the others. It was a shell road called North Project Highway and it extended from Main Street westward almost to Westway Canal. It was a private road and it was owned by one of the oil and gas companies operating in the area. Although the gate was usually left open, there were large *No Trespassing* signs posted all along the property line.

What in the hell are you doing at the end of North Project Highway, Troy Gandy?

CHAPTER 18

11:16 a.m.
North Project Road, Mechant Loup, Louisiana

Baylor had remained with Beth Gandy while Takecia, Amy, and I had driven to the end of North Project Road. Susan had located the contact information for an executive with the oil company and he granted us permission to do whatever we needed to do on their property.

Five minutes after we arrived, Susan met us at the end of the street. She glanced at her phone as she stepped out of her Tahoe. "It's around here somewhere."

I nodded and pointed to where the gravel road ended and where tall grass began. "It looks like the center of the map is at the end of the road."

We all began trudging through the weeds toward the exact spot on the map. We scanned the ground as we walked, trying to see through the thick grass. It would be no easy task, finding this phone.

When we reached the spot on the map, I scanned my surroundings. There was a field to the south, the canal to the west, and a line of trees to the north. I didn't know how deep the trees went, because the leaves were so thick they were impenetrable by the human eye.

"It could be anywhere within fifty yards of this very spot," Susan said, looking over at me. "Want to spread out?"

"I guess we'll have to." I frowned, not knowing where to really begin. It would be nearly impossible to locate the phone in this mess. I suddenly had an idea and pulled out my phone. Scrolling to the text message I'd sent Susan earlier, I obtained Troy's cell number and called it. As it rang in my ear, I asked if anyone could hear it.

Their ears seemed to perk up and they began roving around, listening for the sound of the ring while also pushing blades of weeds apart to peer through to the ground below. I headed toward the ditch that separated the grass path from the wooded area and began following it toward the canal, calling Troy's number again and again.

Takecia and Amy had fanned out across the field to the south and Susan had made her way toward Westway Canal, zigzagging along the grassy road. I had walked the same direction but followed the ditch closely. I hadn't heard or seen anything by the time we reached the canal. We had been out there an hour and were no closer to finding the phone than when we first arrived.

Susan and I met near the edge of Westway Canal. Her tanned skin glistened in the sunlight and there were tiny specks of white and yellow plant debris stuck to the sweat on her arms. My own arms were sweating—as well as every other part of my body—and they burned from the dozens of tiny cuts I'd sustained from pushing through blackberry bushes.

Susan scowled as we glanced out over the water. "Do you think Troy's in there?"

"God, I hope not. It would kill his mom."

She suggested I call the phone again. I did, but we heard nothing. Next, I called Baylor to see if anyone had seen or heard from Troy. No one had. It had been seven hours since he was discovered missing, and every additional minute that ticked by worried me more and more.

I wiped a stream of sweat from my forehead and walked across the field to meet Takecia and Amy, who were approaching our location from the south.

"Anything?" I asked when we were close enough to hear each other.

They shook their heads in unison.

"Nothing at all," Amy said. "We didn't hear the phone and we didn't see any evidence to indicate any human being had been out here in forever."

I scanned the area, wondering if we should bring metal detectors out here. Susan was still at the edge of the canal, but she was now on her phone. After about a minute, she pulled it from her ear and walked over to meet us back at the original pinging spot.

"They pinged it again and it's still within this area," she said, waving her arm around.

I pointed toward the trees. "That's the only place we haven't checked."

"Let's do it." Susan shoved her phone in her pocket and set off toward the ditch. I moved about ten feet to her right and Takecia and Amy fanned out farther to my right. Keeping a consistent distance between us, we all jumped over the ditch at the same time and began pushing our way through the thick underbrush. I stopped intermittently and called Troy's phone, but we didn't hear anything.

It took us about twenty minutes to push through the initial line of trees, which were about fifty feet deep, and we found ourselves in an open field that was overgrown with wild weeds and bushes. Thistles grew in abundance here and many were taller than me. It was nearly impossible to see the ground at our feet.

"If his phone is on silent, we'll never find it," I said as we all stopped and brushed leaves and picker branches from our clothes. I had to raise my voice so Amy, who was farthest to my right, could hear me. "The foliage is just too thick. You could hide an army in this field."

Susan high-stepped it through the weeds—pushing large stems down with her boots—and made her way to where I stood. Beads of perspiration poured down her face. "Maybe we should walk the tree line and look for signs and tracks that would indicate a person came through here." She swiped at the sweat. "As thick as these weeds are, we should notice something."

I nodded and stared up at the bright sky. It had to be close to two o'clock and going on eight hours missing now. If we didn't find something in the daylight, we'd certainly never find anything at night. "Maybe we need to get some townspeople involved," I said, idly watching some birds circle overhead. "It would take a couple hundred people to search this field thoroughly."

"Say the word and I'll sound the alarm."

I started to say the word when something dawned on me. "Oh, no…that's not good."

"What is it?" Susan asked, following my gaze. She suddenly gasped when she saw the circling birds. "Buzzards!"

CHAPTER 19

My heart sank as I rushed through the tall weeds, using the circling buzzards above as my guide. I ignored the slapping of the thick weeds against my face and the sting from the thistles on my arms. Susan, Amy, and Takecia ran with me, pushing the weeds apart with their arms in an attempt to see farther. I fumbled with my phone as I ran and called Troy's phone again.

Amy shot off to the right and Susan went straight ahead. I veered left and Takecia was between Susan and me.

"There!" Amy shouted, pointing in the direction she was running. "I hear a phone ringing."

We all changed course and followed Amy. Susan slammed into Amy's backside when she suddenly pulled up and hollered that we had a body.

I slowed down and drew to a stop when I reached Amy's side. There, face down on the unforgiving ground, was the body of a young boy who appeared to be Troy's age.

"Oh, my God, no," I said, falling to my knees beside the boy. I pressed my index and middle fingers against his carotid artery. He was cold to the touch and there was no heartbeat. I reached for his hand and tested his fingers gently. They were stiff. He'd been dead for hours, probably since last night. I smashed the button on my phone to call Troy's number again and the phone in the boy's pocket started ringing. "Damn it…his poor mom."

Susan put her hand on my shoulder. "Want me to talk to her?"

I stood to my feet and glanced at the ground around Troy's body. There were breaks in the grass heading southeast that represented a drag path. It was faint, but discernible enough that I didn't need

Gretchen Verdin pointing it out to me.

I turned to Amy. "Can you stay with the body while I get my crime scene kit?"

Brushing her blonde hair out of her eyes, she nodded and glanced at Susan, who stood staring at me. I blinked and apologized to Susan.

"Yes…please, I'd love it if you spoke to Mrs. Gandy."

Susan asked Takecia to wait with Amy and then Susan followed me as I tracked the drag marks through the weeds.

"Are you okay, Clint?" she asked when we were out of earshot of Amy and Takecia.

"I'm fine." My mind was preoccupied with trying to figure out who could've killed this kid—if indeed he had been murdered. I hadn't noticed any obvious wounds on the back of his body and there was no blood along the drag trail. What if this wasn't related to the man in the morgue at all? What if it was an accidental overdose or alcohol poisoning? Back when I was a homicide detective in the City of La Mort, I'd worked a number of such death cases where the friends of the victims had panicked and either dumped the bodies or abandoned the place of death. Of course, Troy's mother claimed he didn't have any friends. If she was correct, I could rule that scenario out immediately.

The drag trail zigzagged through the patch of trees and the ditch, ending at the edge of the shell road east of where our vehicles were parked.

"That explains why I couldn't find anything along the ditch west of here," I said when Susan and I jumped the ditch. "The person who dumped his body stayed on the gravel road."

Susan nodded her agreement. "I'll wait here while you get your stuff. Afterward, I'll notify Beth Gandy."

I frowned and shook my head before hurrying toward my Tahoe. No parent should have to endure such horror. Since it was my case, I knew I should be the one to tell Mrs. Gandy, but I needed time to process the scene and I didn't want her to suffer with uncertainty any longer than she had to. Besides, Susan was much better at delivery than I was, and it would probably be easier on Beth.

Once I reached my Tahoe, I backed it to where Susan was waiting and dragged my crime scene box out of the back cargo area. She gave me a brief kiss on the cheek and told me to wish her luck. It was the worst part of our job, and none of us relished death notifications.

When I returned to Troy's body, I pulled out my camera and began taking pictures. Takecia left to assist Susan and Baylor with anything that came up at the house, and Amy stayed behind to help me process the scene.

After I'd documented everything and bagged Troy's hands, I set the body bag on one side of his body. "Mind giving me a hand?" I asked Amy.

"Sure." She pulled on some gloves and grabbed his feet while I grabbed his hands.

Together, we carefully turned him onto his back. I immediately saw the ligature mark across his throat. His eyes were half closed and his tongue was sticking out. I pushed back each eyelid. Petechiae (tiny hemorrhages) were present on the eyeballs.

"He was strangled," I said.

Amy reached for my camera. "Want me to take a picture while you hold the eyelids open?"

I nodded and thanked her when she'd snapped the photographs. I checked Troy for other injuries, but there were none.

After calling the coroner's office to have them send someone to transport the body, I pulled out evidence bags and collected his property. His wallet was still on him and there were a few bills inside, along with his driver's license, a school identification card, an insurance card, and a raffle ticket from his school. There was also a tiny key in his front left pocket, but there were no numbers on it. Whatever it opened, it couldn't be that important.

Once those items were bagged, I reached in his front right pant pocket and removed his cell phone. Saying a silent prayer it wasn't locked, I pressed the *Home* button twice to open it—it worked! I checked his phone contacts and his mother showed up in his *Favorites* file. I then checked his recent calls. His mom's number appeared dozens of times.

I swiped out of that screen and then clicked on his *Messages* icon. My heart leaped a little when I saw a string of text messages between him and a contact called "Sin", and they were at the top of the list. They were all from last night. I opened them and read from the beginning:

9:02 – Troy: my mom just went to bed
9:02 – Sin: Good!
9:04 – Troy: gonna wait to make sure shes sleep
9:04 – Sin: K
10:11 – Troy: on my way
10:12 – Sin: Yay! Can't wait to see you!
10:35 – Sin: Where are you?

10:43 – Sin: Hey...
10:55 – Sin: Troy!!!
11:16 – Sin: Are you still coming???
11:49 – Sin: Going to bed. :-(

I handed the phone to Amy. "What do you think?"

Her brow furrowed as she read the messages. "It looks like he was going to meet someone."

"And they weren't very far away, because Sin expected him there within about twenty minutes."

Amy shuddered slightly as she pointed to Troy's last message and the one from Sin wondering where he was. "He died between ten-eleven and ten-thirty-five."

"Or he was at least incapacitated between those times." I recorded the phone number associated with Sin's text messages in my notebook and then searched through his pictures, hoping he had captured something relating to his murder. No such luck.

I checked the dates and times on the images. The last picture he'd taken was of a girl with a mesh backpack sitting at what appeared to be a school cafeteria table. There were other kids milling around, but they were blurred out. The focus was on the girl smiling back at him. I turned the picture so Amy could see it. "I bet this is Sin."

"And I bet he was on his way to sin with her when he was killed."

CHAPTER 20

6:18 p.m.

Baylor parked his patrol cruiser on the side of the street and shoved the gearshift in park. He had stood beside Chief Wilson three hours earlier while she delivered the horrifying news about Troy Gandy to Mrs. Gandy. He had watched as the woman fell to her knees in a heap and wept uncontrollably. It made him think of his own mother, who had years ago begged him not to join the military. She'd once revealed that her greatest fear was having someone knock on her door to inform her he'd been killed in combat. That revelation stayed with him throughout his years of service and it haunted him.

Mrs. Gandy was reacting exactly as he'd imagined his own mother would react if she ever received that knock at the door, and it was more than he could take. Overcome with emotion, he had inadvertently dropped to the ground with her and held her as tight as he could. He might've even called her mom in his sobbing attempt at comforting her.

Thinking back to that moment caused his eyes to blur and a tear found its way down his cheek. He quickly swiped at it with his palm, angry at himself for showing emotion on the job. Embarrassed beyond words, he had apologized profusely to Chief Wilson afterward, but she had told him it was okay.

"This job can be extremely sad at times," she'd said in a comforting voice. "I just hope you never get so used to it that it stops affecting you. Emotions and feelings are a good thing. It only becomes a problem when you stop feeling anything at all."

Confused, he had asked her if she'd lost the ability to feel. She hadn't shed a tear as she calmly assisted Mrs. Gandy and her face had been void of emotion.

She had smiled and shook her head. "I've felt—and still feel—a lot of pain in this job," she'd admitted. "I keep it inside while I'm in front of the victims and, if need be, I cry about it later when I'm all alone."

Baylor took a deep breath and blew it out forcefully. He didn't have time to cry right now. He had some work to do.

While Chief Wilson was attending the autopsy with Detective Wolf, he and Amy had been tasked with canvassing the neighborhoods in the area in search of a girl named Sin. It was a weird name, but Chief Wilson had sent a picture of the young girl to their phones and delivered a simple message; "Find her!"

After grabbing his notebook and pen, Baylor stepped out of his patrol car and shined his flashlight at the street sign. It was Dire Lane. He made a note of the name and the time, and then proceeded to knock on doors. He showed the picture to people at the first six houses on either side of the street, but no one knew her. One lady said the girl looked familiar, but she couldn't say for sure.

"Do you have a better picture?" she'd asked.

When Baylor told her no, she'd frowned and said she wished she could help, but she wasn't sure where she'd seen the girl, or even if it was her.

Baylor moved his car to the second block and strode up a long concrete driveway and rang the doorbell at the next house down the street.

A man answered and Baylor went through the motions, asking the man if he'd ever seen the girl before. The man pulled some reading glasses from his pocket and pulled the phone close to his face.

"She looks young." He turned his head and hollered over his shoulder. "Kegan! Come here, son."

A few seconds later a short kid with dark hair appeared from a back hallway. He approached the door with apprehension when he saw Baylor in uniform.

"What's up, Dad?"

The man handed him Baylor's phone. "Do you know this girl? She looks familiar."

"Yeah," the boy said, seemingly relieved Baylor wasn't there for him. "That's Burton's adopted sister."

"Do you know her name?" Baylor asked, his pen poised over his notepad and his heart thumping with excitement. This was the first major case he'd been involved with and he might've just cracked it.

"Yeah, it's Cindy. Cindy Vincent." The kid cracked a wise-ass smile. "She's not really adopted. Burton just says so to piss her off."

Baylor stifled a chuckle. "Where do they live?"

Kegan gave Baylor back his phone and shot a thumb toward the back of the street. "Third to last on the right," he said. "Is Cindy finally going to jail for annoying Burton?"

"Not quite, big man," Baylor said, resisting the urge to call him "little" due to his height—or lack thereof. "Thanks a bunch, though. It's much appreciated."

As Baylor drove to the back of the street, he called Chief Wilson and told her what he'd found.

"Good work!" she said. "Make contact with her and let her know the Chief of Detectives is on his way."

Before Baylor could answer, he heard Detective Wolf's voice in the background saying, "Stop calling me that! My name's Clint."

He ended the call and made a mental note to call him Clint from now on. He didn't want to piss the man off. He knew there was a lot he could learn from him and he didn't want to start off on Clint's bad side.

Baylor pulled into the driveway of the third to last house on the right and stepped from his patrol cruiser. He didn't know the girl's connection to the case, so he kept his hand close to his holster and surveyed his surroundings as he approached the raised house. When he'd first rolled into Louisiana he'd asked why so many houses were built high off the ground, and he'd been given a simple answer: floods.

He strode up the flight of wooden steps and knocked on the door, then stepped to one side. A man appeared in the doorway and smiled.

"Hello, officer, what can I do for you?"

After introducing himself and learning that the man's name was Rick Vincent, Baylor explained he was there to make contact with his daughter, Cindy. "Our Chief of Detectives, Clint Wolf, will be by shortly to question her."

The man scowled. "Cindy? Are you sure you don't mean Burton?"

"I'm certain," Baylor said. "It's about her boyfriend."

"Her boyfriend, eh?" Rick's face hardened a little. "Please come in, Officer Rice. I'll call Cindy down and we can wait for Chief Wolf together. I think I might also have a few questions for Cindy."

CHAPTER 21

Twenty-eight minutes later…

I parked my Tahoe behind Baylor's patrol cruiser and hurried up the steps to the Vincent home. My mind was racing. How did this young girl factor into Troy's murder? The coroner had ruled the cause of death as asphyxiation due to ligature strangulation and the manner of death was a homicide. The ligature marks were consistent with quarter-inch wire or rope of some sort, but the marks were deep, which indicated some amount of force was used. There had been a little blood within the ligature marks, and the doctor thought a piece of rough wire was more likely the murder weapon, rather than a piece of rope.

Was Cindy Vincent strong enough to overpower Troy Gandy and strangle him? Did she have access to a piece of rough wire? If she was involved with Troy's murder, how did that relate to the shooting death of our unidentified victim? There were so many questions, but no answers.

I had dropped Susan off at the police department before heading here, and I texted her to let her know I'd arrived. I then rapped loudly on the door and waited. The front door was solid metal and I couldn't see inside, but there was light coming through the window to the right and I saw shadows moving toward the door.

When it opened, Rick Vincent and Baylor stepped out onto the wooden porch. Rick shook my hand.

"It's been a long time, detective," he joked, but he sounded a little nervous.

"Yeah, I wasn't expecting to see you again so soon."

"What's going on…exactly?" he asked. "I didn't even know my daughter had a boyfriend, and now Officer Rice here tells me you need to question her. To be quite honest, I'm a bit disappointed in her, but I'm also a little scared. Is this kid involved in something sinister? Should my family and I be worried? There was that body in the canal and now this…" His voice trailed off and he shook his head slowly. "I'm scared for my family, detective."

"I'm not sure how—or if—the body in the canal has anything to do with what's happening here, but I need to sit down with your daughter and ask her some questions."

"But what's going on with this kid—this Gandy fellow?"

I didn't want to say too much too soon, so I went with the initial report. "His mother called our office this morning and reported him missing. I was hoping your daughter might know what he was up to last night."

"I can't believe she was dating behind our backs." He frowned. "You raise your kids to do the right thing, but you never know what can happen…you know what I mean?"

I nodded. "So, do you mind bringing Cindy down to the police department?"

"Down to the department?" He was thoughtful. "Can't you just question her here? I'm pulling a weekend shift at work and have to be there by four in the morning."

"I'd rather do it at the office where I have my recording equipment," I said. "It shouldn't take too long. I'll take her statement and then send her on her way."

Rick hesitated for a moment. Finally, he asked if Cindy was in trouble.

"Not at all." I tried to sound reassuring. *At least, not at the moment.* "I simply need to ask her if she knew what his plans were for last night and today."

"Let me speak with Judith. She might be able to bring her for me." He turned and disappeared into the house. After a minute or two, he returned with Judith, Cindy, and Burton.

"Judith will take her," Rick said. "Is it okay if my son rides along?"

I shrugged. "I'm fine with it."

"I don't know why I have to go," Burton grumbled. "I wasn't dating the loser."

"That's enough, Burt," Judith snapped, pushing her long brown hair out of her face in angry fashion. "Cindy doesn't want to go either, but she's got no choice."

I thought about correcting her and telling her I couldn't legally force Cindy to come to the station if she didn't want to, but decided against it. If I corrected Judith, she might refuse to bring Cindy—and who was I to regulate her assumptions, anyway?

As Judith and her children walked to the black Jeep Grand Cherokee parked under the carport, Rick called out from the porch and thanked me for my rapid response on Monday. "The boys told me you didn't waste any time getting here. I really appreciate it. It's good to know we live in a community where the law can get here at the drop of a hat."

I waved my thanks and then turned to Baylor when we reached the edge of the concrete driveway. "You can head home if you like. It's been a long day."

"I thought I'd go to the office and get my report done first—while things are still fresh in my mind."

I liked his initiative. "I appreciate your help today, Baylor."

"Are you kidding?" he said. "I love this stuff. It beats writing tickets any day."

I thanked him again and backed my Tahoe out of the driveway so he could leave. I then pulled forward and waited for Judith to back out of the driveway. Once her headlights were shining in my rearview mirror, I headed for the office. I caught glimpses of Judith's and Cindy's faces as we passed under the street lights along Dire Lane. It looked like Judith was scolding Cindy, who just sat with her head buried in her hands. It looked like she was crying.

I was turning down Washington Avenue when Susan called.

"Where are you?" she asked.

"A mile from the office."

"Did Cindy agree to come in?"

"Yep...she's right behind me with her mother."

"Mind if I sit in on the interview?"

"I'd love it."

There was a brief pause, where I heard her take a deep breath, and then she said, "Do you remember the lady with the little boy named Sammy?"

"From Bad Loup Burgers?"

"She's the one."

"Considering it only happened yesterday and I haven't been beaten in the head like you have, I do remember."

"Well, her name is Allie and she's in the hospital."

"What?" I nearly smashed the brakes in shock. "What happened? Is she okay?"

"It was her husband…Jake Boudreaux. He was angry because Sammy said some nice man bought them lunch, so he took an old Stillson wrench to her ribs and legs. She's messed up bad—can't walk."

"No…" My heart sank to my boots. Guilt suddenly turned to anger and I cursed out loud. "Where is this prick?"

"He's on the loose. Melvin swore out a warrant for him and he's looking for him right now. He thinks the prick left town, but as soon as we're done with Cindy Vincent, I'm going to stay out and help him look for Jake."

Any normal husband would probably worry about his wife in a situation like this, but I wasn't. While police work was dangerous and I did worry about her in general, I knew Susan was more than capable of taking care of herself. I'd often said the safest place in town was right next to her.

"What about Sammy?" I asked. "Where is he and how's he doing?"

"He's with his grandparents—Allie's mom and dad. He's fine, but Jake slapped him and left a mark on his cheek."

I squeezed the steering wheel so hard I thought I'd snap it. I wanted to get my hands on Jake Boudreaux something fierce. "I'll stay out and help y'all look for him," I said. "And I hope to find him first."

CHAPTER 22

Cindy Vincent's orange freckles glistened brightly in the tears that streamed down her cheeks. They matched the color of her hair. She had taken a seat in one of the visitor's chairs in my office and I sat in the other chair beside her. Susan sat behind my desk and was prepared to take notes for me.

"It's okay," I said to Cindy in as soothing a voice as I could manage. "You're not in any trouble. I promise. I just need your help in finding out what Troy Gandy was up to last night."

"I don't know anything about him."

"Before we get to that, let me ask some basic questions." I then proceeded to ask her for her age, date of birth, address, home phone number, and then her cell phone number. She provided all of it and I noticed immediately that her cell phone number matched the one in Troy's phone that was assigned to "Sin".

"Is it true that you and Troy Gandy were dating?"

She shook her head. "I heard that cop tell my dad we were dating, but that's not true. I'm not allowed to date anyone. I barely even know him."

"When was the last time you heard from Troy yesterday?"

"I already said I don't know anything about him." She was staring down at her hands and wouldn't look up at me.

"Well, when's the last time you saw him?"

"Like *talked* to him or just *saw* him?"

"Saw him."

"Yesterday at school."

"When's the last time you talked to him?"

"I don't talk to him."

I frowned, not wanting to interrogate this young girl. It would be emotionally scarring enough to learn that her boyfriend had been murdered, and I didn't want to make it worse by forcing the truth out of her. I leaned close and asked if she would look at me. She slowly lifted her head.

"Listen, Cindy...I know you were dating Troy and I know he was supposed to meet you last night. I have his phone and I know you're listed as S-i-n in his contacts." I paused to let that information sink in, and her chin slowly began to quiver. "I need to know if he made it to your house."

"I don't know what you're talking about," Cindy said weakly. "I don't talk to Troy."

"I'm aware your parents don't know about your relationship with Troy, and I know he's been sneaking in your room at night. That's not my concern and your personal information will stay in this room"—I waved my hand around—"between the three of us. I simply need to know if he made it to your house last night."

Cindy shifted in her chair and brushed some tears away from her face. "Why are you even asking me about Troy? Did he do something wrong?"

"No, young lady, he didn't do anything wrong," I said slowly. "Something bad happened to him."

She gasped out loud. "What? What happened to him?"

"Don't you know?"

"No! What happened?"

"Did he make it to your house last night?"

"No, okay! He didn't make it to my house." Cindy spat the words, and tears sprayed from her mouth as she spoke. "He texted me and told me he was coming, but he never made it. Now, what happened to him?"

"I need you to prepare yourself, okay?" I paused and stared into her bloodshot eyes. "Troy was found in a field north of his house."

Cindy stared blankly at me. "What was he doing in a field? Was he lost? Did he go the wrong way?"

"No."

"Well, what happened?"

"Someone hurt him, Cindy. They hurt him and left him in a field."

"How...but...is he okay? How bad is he hurt?"

"He's gone, Cindy. He's gone."

I wasn't prepared for how she'd react. She jumped to her feet and screamed in my face. The veins in her neck bulged and her eyes nearly bugged out of her head. I stood and reached out for her shoulders, but she pushed me and ran for the door, trying desperately to work the knob.

Susan was on Cindy in a flash and wrapped her arms around her, trying to keep her from flailing about and hurting herself.

"It's okay, sweetie, I've got you," Susan said calmly. "Go ahead and cry…let it all out."

I heard some excited chatter from the lobby area and I brushed by Susan and Cindy to deal with Judith Vincent. When I stepped into the lobby, she and Burton were on their feet.

"What did you do to my daughter?" Judith asked in an accusing tone. "Why is she crying? What did you do?"

"This fellow, Troy Gandy—"

"She already said she wasn't dating anyone and I believe her!"

"I understand, but… Well, ma'am, we found Troy dead this afternoon," I explained. "She freaked out when we told her."

"Why would she freak out? She said she doesn't even know the kid."

"You'll have to ask her that question," I said flatly.

"She does know him, Ma," Burton said in a hoarse voice. "He's been by the house when you and Dad were at work."

Judith whirled on him. "*What?* And you never told us? That's it—you're grounded until your twentieth birthday, boy! I can't believe you would keep something like this from us!"

"She threatened me." Burton threw up his hands as though to say, "*What was I supposed to do?*"

Judith started to yell at Burton again, but I stepped forward. "Ma'am, you're going to have to lower your voice if you want to remain in this building. I understand you're upset, but you'd better get a hold of yourself."

Her mouth dropped open in shock and then slowly clamped shut as she realized I wasn't smiling.

"Now, your daughter's upset and she's going to need you to be calm."

"I want to see her."

"I understand, but can you just give us a few more minutes with her? Troy was supposed to meet her at your house last night and we need to know if he showed up or not."

She rubbed her face and then began digging in her purse. "I need to call Rick. He should be here."

"Good idea," I said. "I'll finish taking Cindy's statement and then she'll be free to go."

I closed the lobby door behind me and strode to my office. Cindy was back sitting in the chair and wasn't screaming anymore, but she was crying hysterically.

"I…I don't understand," she wailed. "I just spoke to him last night. He was fine."

"Are you sure he didn't make it to your house?" I asked.

"I'm positive. He texted me saying he was on his way. It usually only takes him about ten minutes to ride his bike to my house, but he never showed up. I texted him to see where he was, but he never answered." She shuddered violently. "I…I just figured his mom woke up and he couldn't leave or maybe she caught him leaving and took his phone away. That's how she usually punishes him—by taking away his phone."

"You said he rides his bike to your house. Where does he park it?"

"He hides it behind my dad's garage, in between these two big drums that are back there."

I nodded and glanced at Susan to see if she had any questions. She frowned and shook her head, still with one arm wrapped tightly around Cindy. We all sat quietly for a few moments, with nothing but the sound of Cindy's sniffling filling the room. After a long few minutes, Cindy asked how Troy had been killed.

"Was he shot?" she asked, her voice still quivering.

"No," I said. "Why do you want to know if he was shot?"

Cindy recounted a story of how Troy had gone to her house to visit while Burton and his friends were there. "Troy was going in my room so we could study and Burt threatened to shoot him."

I felt my ears perk up. "Really? When was this?"

"The same day he and his friends found that man in the canal. They were bullying Troy when he came to visit me and Burton said he had the green light to shoot him if he came in my room."

"You don't really think Burton would hurt another kid, do you?" I asked.

Cindy shrugged. "He set the neighbor's hay bales on fire."

CHAPTER 23

After escorting Cindy to the lobby with her mom, I turned to Burton. "Why don't you come with me for a minute?" I said. "I've got a few questions for you."

"Me?" Burton turned from me to his sister. He sneered when they locked eyes. "I didn't do anything wrong, so why am I being called in?"

"Burt, do what you're told," Judith said. "Don't make me call your dad."

Grumbling to himself, Burton stood and followed me to my office. I pointed to the chair next to Susan and he fell into it. He tried to look tough and unbothered by the fact that he was in a police station being questioned, but I could see beyond the façade.

"So, as you're already aware, Troy Gandy was found dead," I began. "I was hoping you could help us figure out what happened to him."

Burton shrugged. "I've got no idea what happened to him. All I know is that he was dating my sister without my dad's permission. He'd come to the house after school before my parents would get home and they'd go in her room and close the door."

"Did you know that he was sneaking in Cindy's window at night?"

That got his attention. "What?"

"Does that make you mad?" I stared him right in the eye and watched as he fidgeted in his chair.

"I don't really care what Cindy does."

"Is that so? Then why'd you threaten to shoot Troy when he went in Cindy's room?"

"That's a lie!" Burton's mouth dropped open in feigned disbelief and he shot a thumb toward the lobby. "Did she tell you that? Because I can prove it didn't happen. I never made any threats to Troy. I was nice to him."

"How can you prove it?" I asked.

"I can get Kegan to come tell you what happened. He was there and saw the whole thing."

"Oh, Kegan...he was with you when you found our victim."

Burton nodded. "That's the one. He can tell you what happened. If anything, Troy threatened me."

I nodded slowly and reached for the file folder at the far corner of my desk. I dug in it until I found the envelope containing the memory card with the crime scene photos. I shoved it in the SD port on my computer and fired it up. Once I found the picture of Troy's phone, I swung my monitor around so Burton could see it.

"Do you know what that is?" I asked.

He shrugged. "A smart phone."

"Not just *any* smart phone—it's Troy's smart phone." I minimized the picture and rested my elbows on the desk. "Would it surprise you if I said Troy recorded the conversation between you and him on his phone?"

Burton hesitated and I saw his Adam's apple move vertically as he swallowed hard. I knew I had him.

"Sure, I can call Kegan down here and question him. He might even lie for you." I placed my hands flat on the desk and spread my fingers. "But who do you think a jury would believe—you and your friend or an actual recording?"

"I...I didn't." Burton gulped again. "I didn't threaten him."

"Look," I said, waving dismissively, "if you were messing around and said you were going to shoot him as a joke—just to scare him so he wouldn't be mean to your sister—that's one thing. But if you're going to sit here and lie about it, I've got to think the threat was credible and you did something to carry it out. Maybe you caught him parking his bicycle behind the garage and you took matters into your own hands. Maybe you started arguing at first and everything just happened so fast. It was an accident, perhaps."

Burton's eyes were growing wider and wider. Although I wouldn't have thought it possible, his face grew even whiter than it was normally. "I didn't do anything to him!"

"How can I believe you about the murder when you won't tell the truth about the threat?"

"I didn't do it." His voice had lost its bravado. I thought he was about to start crying.

"Like I said, I want to believe you, but I can't as long as you continue to lie." I leaned back and folded my arms across my chest, studying him with cold eyes. "Have you ever wondered what it'd be like to spend the rest of your life in prison?"

Burton gasped. "No!"

"Well, you'd better start thinking about it and making preparations, because that'll be your future if you weren't joking with Troy."

"I didn't threaten him!"

"Were you planning to shoot him if you caught him on your property again?"

"No!" He shook his head violently from side to side.

"Were you planning to kill him in some other way if you caught him sneaking into your sister's room?"

"No, sir!"

"So, it was all a joke?"

"Yes, sir!" The instant he said it, he realized he had just admitted to making the threat. His shoulders drooped. "I would never hurt anyone. I swear it."

"Why were you joking with him?"

Burton shrugged. "I don't know. I guess I was just trying to protect my sister."

"Would you hurt anyone to protect her?"

He shook his head again. "I'd never hurt anyone—and I definitely wouldn't kill a person."

I continued studying him. He seemed to finally be telling the truth, but I wanted to test him a little more. "Remember when your neighbor's hay bales caught fire on New Years?"

He sighed heavily. "Yes, sir."

"Who did that?"

"I did, but it was an accident. I was shooting off some bottle rockets and one of them went crazy and landed in the hay. I tried to put out the fire, but it spread too fast."

Burton was relaxed now. The tension had left his face and he was breathing normally. It was my guess he was finally being truthful. "Any idea what could've happened to Troy?"

"I don't know about Troy, but Kegan and Paulie and I were talking about the floating man yesterday at school." He looked up. "You know, trying to figure out what happened to him."

Sometimes clues came from the damnedest places. "Well, what'd y'all come up with?"

He hesitated and licked his lips. He opened his mouth to speak, but then stopped. I knew something was on his mind.

"What is it, Burt?" I used the nickname his mom had used, trying to make him feel at ease with me. "What are you trying to tell me?"

"It was Kegan's idea, but Paulie and I were against it from the beginning." Burton took a deep breath and exhaled. "We—well, me and Paulie—think it had something to do with the phone call."

"What phone call?" I glanced sideways at Susan. She was leaning forward in her chair and her expression appeared as curious as I felt.

"Back in August, right before school started, Paulie and his family went on vacation to Gatlinburg, Tennessee," Burton explained. "Paulie got a gift for Kegan and a gift for me. Well, his mom and dad paid for Kegan's gift, but mine didn't cost anything. Kegan got this cool tomahawk, but I got a piece of paper. It was some kind of missing person poster or something. There was a woman and a boy on it and they had disappeared or something. They were endangered, I think." He paused and thought back. He nodded his head. "Yeah, I'm pretty sure it said they were in some kind of danger.

"Anyhow, when Paulie saw the missing person poster on the wall by this shop, he thought the boy looked like me and the lady looked like my mom, so he swiped it."

Burton paused again and I frowned, wondering where he was going with this story. What did a flyer in Gatlinburg have to do with a man floating in Westway Canal?

"Paulie's mom had to go to Mechant Groceries later that day, so we all tagged along. We waited in the car at first, but then we saw a payphone and Kegan thought it would be funny to call the number on the poster. We tried to talk him out of it, but he insisted on doing it, so we walked to the payphone with him and watched him make the call."

I scowled, disappointed. I had been expecting more from his story. "Is that it?"

"He called the number on the poster and said he knew where the missing family was and that he wanted a reward or they'd never find them. The next thing we know, there's a dead guy in the canal behind our house." Burton blinked. "I don't think that's a coincidence."

I ran through a number of scenarios in my head, none of which made sense. "I don't know, Burt. Why would someone come all the way out here to kill somebody just because of a phone call?"

"I don't know," Burton said, "but they did."

I was thoughtful. I glanced over at Susan and she only shrugged.

"Where's the poster?" I asked.

"It was hanging on the refrigerator by a magnet but I can't find it. I think Cindy threw it away. She's always messing with my stuff. I looked everywhere, but I haven't been able to locate it."

"Do you remember the number Kegan called?"

Burton shook his head. "We didn't want to call on our cell phones, because we thought we'd get in trouble for making a prank call. That's why we used the payphone."

I smiled wryly. "So, you admit that you went along with it?"

"Huh?"

"Earlier you said you and Paulie tried to talk Kegan out of doing it, but you just acknowledged having a part in it."

He sighed again. "Okay, you got me. We thought it would be funny at first, but that man turned up dead and then we saw the picture of the truck in the newspaper. We figured it all had to be connected. It scared the crap out of us."

I drummed my fingers on the desk for about a minute. Finally, I asked if he remembered anything at all about the poster. "Names, dates, locations, descriptions…anything at all?"

He shook his head. "I just remember thinking the boy didn't look like me at all. Paulie and Kegan thought so, but I didn't."

"What did they look like, the woman and boy?"

"They both had brown hair and brown eyes and their complexion was light, but that's about as close as they came to looking like me and my mom."

"What day did the phone call happen?"

Burton scowled. "I don't really remember. You'd have to ask Paulie's mom."

It was my turn to sigh. "Okay, if you remember anything— anything at all—you let me know."

Susan and I stood and walked him to the lobby and told Judith they were free to go.

"We would like to search your back yard and the area around your garage," I said, indicating with my head toward Cindy. "Just in case Troy made it to your house and hid his bicycle in the back of the garage."

"Sure…no problem." Judith looked at Burton and then at Susan and me. "Is Burt in any trouble?"

"No, ma'am," I said. "He might've actually helped us out again."

"Are you kidding me?" Cindy panted in exasperation, her eyes still swollen from crying. "How does he keep getting away with everything?"

CHAPTER 24

Susan rode with me as we followed Judith Vincent and her children to Dire Lane. After making contact with Rick at his house, we obtained permission to search his back yard and, flashlights in hand, headed for the garage. Rick turned on a bank of floodlights that hung from the soffit along the western side of the house. "Feel free to search inside the garage, too," he called from the back porch, "just in case Troy hid his bicycle in there."

I waved my thanks and we searched the back of the detached garage first. The siding on the garage didn't match the siding on the house and neither did the roof. "I guess this was an aftermarket garage," I said.

Susan only nodded, as she shined her light behind the two drums positioned along the back side of the garage. They were exactly where Cindy said they would be, but there was no bicycle. I shined my light around the yard. Four chairs were situated around a fire pit at the center of the back yard, a swing stood alone in the far corner, and an aboveground swimming pool was set up near the house. Nothing appeared disturbed.

"It doesn't look like he made it here," Susan said as we opened the side door to the garage and stepped inside. There was nothing but a red Ford Mustang in the garage, along with some tools, a riding mower, a push mower, and other miscellaneous items.

I suddenly remembered Mr. Pellegrin and his cameras at the front of the street. I snapped my fingers. "First thing tomorrow morning I'm going to check with Mr. Pellegrin and view his cameras. If Troy rode his bike down this street, we'll definitely know it."

Susan and I closed up the garage and thanked Rick Vincent.

Next, we made contact with Kegan Davis and his parents, and then Paul Rupe and his parents. Both boys verified what Burton had said, and neither of them remembered anything about the missing person poster other than what we already knew. Paul's mom remembered it being Saturday, August 6 when they went to Mechant Groceries.

"We got home from vacation on Friday night," she said, "and I went to the store the next morning. I remembered them hanging out by the payphone, but I had no idea what they were up to."

"What time did y'all go to the store?" I asked.

She was thoughtful. "It had to be nine or ten, because I started cooking lunch when I got back home."

Paul remembered stripping the poster from the wall outside of a candy apple store on the strip in Gatlinburg, but he couldn't remember anything more.

"The people on it just looked a lot like Burton and his mom, so I took it and gave it to him," Paul said. "I didn't read it or anything." After hesitating briefly, he said, "I hope I'm not in any trouble. I mean, it's not like I stole something. It was just a piece of paper."

I let him know he wasn't in trouble and, after asking a few more questions, Susan and I left. I dropped Susan off at the police department so she could get her Tahoe, and then followed her home. Damian Conner's truck was parked in front of the gym and he was sitting on his tailgate. In the glow from the streetlight overhead, I could see that his arms were folded and his jaw was set.

"Looks like you're in trouble," I told Susan when I stepped out of my truck and met her in the driveway. Damian had scooted off the tailgate and was heading our way. "Do you think he'll make you run laps?"

Ignoring my comments, Susan gave a cheerful wave. "Hey, Uncle D, how's it going?"

"Considering I've been waiting here since six..." He stopped when he reached us and shoved his fists against his hips. His left eyelid usually drooped low—no doubt a byproduct of being punched in the face too many times—but it was opened wide at the moment. "You owe me two hours of hard work before you get to have some sleep."

I chuckled inwardly, turning slowly toward Susan. *This'll be good.*

"Yes, sir," she said. "I'll get dressed and be out in a minute."

I did a double-take and watched her turn abruptly and walk to the house. My mouth must've been hanging open, because Damian laughed. "What's the matter, son? She doesn't listen to you like that?"

"If I ever spoke to her like that, she would probably do a flying arm-bar and snap my elbow in half."

"Well," said the man of few words. "It was good chatting, but I need to open the gym."

I glanced at my phone. It was nine o'clock. Instead of sticking around to watch Susan train, I decided to head to the shelter and finish up what little work was left to be done. Susan was hoping for an October opening, and I wanted to make sure she got it.

We passed each other in the hall and I told her I was heading to the shelter. "I'll see you when I get back."

"I don't know," she said. "He looks pissed, so I might not make it."

We both laughed and I quickly dressed into some old shorts and a T-shirt. I called for Achilles to jump in the front seat of my truck and we headed for the back of the property. There was no moon shining overhead and everything was cloaked in utter darkness, save for my stabbing headlights.

When I broke free from the rows of sugarcane that lined either side of the road, I parked in front of the shelter and shut off my engine. I stepped out of the truck and held the door for Achilles. As soon as he hit the ground, he was off. Something had attracted his attention—probably a rabbit or an armadillo—and he was on a search-and-destroy mission.

As I walked up the steps, I considered this place and suddenly remembered Allie Boudreaux and her little boy, Sammy. I pulled out my phone and called Melvin.

"What's up, Chief?" he asked cheerfully.

"You have to stop calling me that, Melvin."

"It's habit."

"Well, it makes Susan uncomfortable," I lied, knowing that would get his attention.

"What? Really?" He began stammering. "Gee, look, please tell her I'm sorry. I had no idea. I won't do it again."

I broke out laughing and he cursed.

"Are you messing with me?" he asked.

"That's for you to figure out," I said, then sobered up. "Look, I'm calling to see if you found Jake Boudreaux yet."

"No." Melvin sighed. "I've looked everywhere. I think he left town. I put out a BOLO to the sheriff's office in case they run across him."

"How's Allie?"

"Last I heard, she was doing better. Still in a lot of pain, but better."

I thanked him and ended the call, wondering if she and Sammy might become Susan's first clients.

CHAPTER 25

Saturday, October 1

I was up bright and early in the morning and drove straight to the Pellegrin residence. I'd spent most of the night cleaning up the shelter, arranging furniture, and installing switch and receptacle wall plates. Things were looking good. Susan had met me at the shelter after her training and, although she was tired, had moved from bedroom to bedroom putting bright new sheets on the beds. We left the place at two in the morning and I'd gotten a little more than three hours of sleep before my alarm went off.

I didn't drink coffee often, but figured I'd need one today, so I bought a cup on my way to the Pellegrin residence. I took a long swig before stepping out of my Tahoe. I winced as the steaming liquid hit the back of my throat and seemed to burn a hole right through it.

"That'll leave a mark," I said out loud, my voice sounding hoarse. I grabbed my notepad and strode quickly up the driveway. While it was clear outside and the sun was just starting to rise, it had to be less than sixty degrees. There wasn't much of a breeze, but when the wind did stir, it was cool and felt good against my face. I wondered if this meant we were finally going to experience fall-like weather.

I knocked on the door and Mr. Pellegrin answered wearing the same pajamas he'd worn on the first night I met him. Had I not seen him on his way to work that one morning, I'd be convinced these pajamas were all he wore.

"Mr. Pellegrin, how are you?" I smiled wide. "I told you I'd be back for more footage, and here I am."

"Well, come on in then," he said, pulling the door wider to make room for me to enter. He began complaining about the approaching Presidential election as we walked to his bedroom. He led the way to a cluttered room and, while things were strewn all about, it was hard to miss the pump-action shotgun leaning in the corner near the head of the bed. "I keep the system in here," he explained, "because a criminal would have to come through me to get to it, and"—he shoved his thumb in the direction of the shotgun—"that won't happen."

He walked to a roll-top desk opposite the bed and shoved the top up, exposing a monitor and hard drive.

"Nice." I whistled in appreciation, making a mental note to talk to Susan about setting up high-quality cameras around the shelter. "This is a great setup."

Mr. Pellegrin nodded and pointed to a stool that was propped against the wall. "Drag that over here and have a seat while I pull up the footage. What days and times are we looking at?"

Troy Gandy had left his house around ten o'clock on Thursday night, but I asked Mr. Pellegrin to start at nine o'clock.

The elderly man's movements were measured, but it seemed as though he knew what he was doing. In one of the split screens to the left, I could see my Tahoe parked in his driveway. He clicked something and all of the screens went blank. I heard a little grunt and I looked up at his face. His busy white eyebrows came together above the bridge of his nose. "That's strange," he mumbled to himself.

"What's strange?" I asked, not liking the way he was acting.

He didn't answer. Instead, he kept moving the cursor around with the mouse and clicking different features. He clicked a button that read, *Playback*, and then a calendar appeared at the bottom right of the screen. He clicked on Thursday's date, but an error message appeared stating that the playback failed and no records matched his request.

"This doesn't make sense."

I began to sweat as he maneuvered the cursor around the screen and clicked on the live view. He then grunted and his shoulders fell. "Damn it! I forgot to set it back to record."

My own shoulders fell. "What? It wasn't recording?"

He shook his head. "I'm sorry, detective, but I forgot to set it back to record when I made the copies for you."

I wanted to groan out loud, but I resisted the urge. After all, it wasn't his job to catch a killer for me.

He clicked on the *record* button and said, "Okay, now they're recording. If you need any more footage, I'll have it."

I needed Thursday night's footage! I wanted to scream, but didn't. I thanked him and trudged out into the cool morning air. I walked to the edge of his driveway and looked up and down Dire Lane. Troy Gandy might've ridden his bicycle right in front of this house—but I'd never know it.

CHAPTER 26

After leaving Mr. Pellegrin's house, I drove to Mechant Groceries. It was a newer building that had gone up at the corner of a large sugarcane field. The concrete parking area and the foundation upon which the store was built took up about 200,000 square feet of land. More and more, it seemed progress was pushing the cane farmers onto smaller and smaller tracts of land, and I wondered what would happen if they were someday pushed out of existence. I certainly wouldn't be happy, because thick cane syrup was my favorite pancake topping.

I got a parking spot close to the store and walked inside, making a mental note of the location of the payphone and the surveillance camera as I walked by. It wasn't very busy at that time of the morning. I hooked a left and stopped at the service desk.

"Can I help you?" asked a young girl who appeared to be a high school student.

I smiled. "Yes, ma'am. I need to speak with a manager."

She lifted a handset from its cradle and dialed a four-digit number. "Miss Cassandra, there's a detective asking for you." She quickly shook her head. "No, not by name—he's just asking to speak with a manager."

When the girl returned the handset to the cradle, she smiled and said the manager would be right down. Before the words left her mouth, there was movement from an elevated office behind the counter. On my side of the wall to the office and just behind the young cashier, there were five shelves extending from one end to the other, left to right, and they were filled with every kind of liquor one could imagine. I saw a variety of vodka bottles and felt an urging in my gut to have a drink.

Blinking quickly, I turned away and focused my attention above the top of the wall, where a short stocky girl was lumbering down the stairs. She disappeared for a brief moment and then reappeared around the corner to the left. She stopped when she reached the young girl. Her shirt had the name *Cassandra* and the title *Weekend Manager* embroidered on it.

I introduced myself and asked if we could speak in her office. She hesitated, glancing down at the badge clipped to my belt and the gun on my hip.

"You're not in any trouble," I said. "I just have to ask some questions about a customer."

That seemed to reassure her. She lifted a section of hinged countertop and let me through to her side. She then led the way up a flight of stairs and into a square office that overlooked the store aisles below. Cassandra sat at the desk and folded her hands in her lap. "What do you need from me?"

"I'd like to look at surveillance footage from August sixth, between nine and ten o'clock in the morning…the camera overlooking the payphones. I need to know the exact time a particular call was made from the payphone."

Cassandra's eyes narrowed. "You're the second person in two weeks to ask to see that footage. There must be something very important on there."

"Really?" I cocked my head sideways. "Who was the other person?"

"Some man with a badge who said he needed to see the tapes because of a case he was investigating."

"What kind of case was it?"

She shrugged. "I don't know."

"You didn't ask?"

"No…and I didn't ask you either. I just assume it's not my business."

Good point. "Did he volunteer any information at all?"

"He said he got a call from the payphone and he wanted to see who made that call."

My heart began to beat in my chest, as I figured I was finally on to something. Could this be the guy they called? Had he tracked them down? If so, was he our dead guy? Or did he have something to do with shooting the dead guy? "Did this man say what date and time it was when he received the call from the payphone?"

She was thoughtful. "He did give me an exact date and time, but I don't remember. I wrote it down on a sticky note, but that's long gone. I do think it was in the morning sometime, though."

"Did he say what the call was about?"

She shook her head.

I drummed my fingers on the desk. "What did the man look like?"

"He was taller than me and a little stocky. He had an accent—that much I know."

"What kind of accent?"

"Like he was from Alabama or something."

I jotted that down in my notes and then pointed to the monitor hanging on the wall above the surveillance equipment console. "Can I see the footage from the payphone?"

She grimaced and sucked air in through her teeth. It made a whistling sound that was annoying. "Oh, did you say the sixth of August?"

I nodded.

She turned to a calendar on the wall and, flipping back to August, began counting from the sixth to today. "It's over forty-five days, so we won't have it. Our system will record over itself every forty-five days—sometimes sooner."

I wanted to curse my luck out loud, but didn't. I dropped my notepad on the desk and leaned back in my chair. What would it take to catch a break in this case? As I stared at the ceiling thinking, I suddenly had an idea. I leaned forward. "What day did this man come in the store?"

Cassandra stared at the calendar, as though she thought it would speak to her. Finally, she nodded. "It was the eighteenth—two Sundays ago. He came in about twelve-ten."

It was only thirteen days ago, but I was impressed that she remembered the exact time he came in. I asked how she could remember that small detail.

"I only remember because the Saints were playing and I was up here in my office listening to the start of the game. They had just kicked off when I was called to go down and speak to the man. He stayed here for over an hour, so I missed a big part of the game." She shook her head. "I was so mad! And then they lost and that just ruined my whole day."

I smiled, and then asked to see the footage from when the man came to the store.

"Sure," she said. "I'll do it, but just as long as we're done before tomorrow at three-twenty-five, because I ain't missing another game for this payphone."

I nodded and watched as she began working the surveillance system. I couldn't help but wonder who would appear on the screen. Would I finally be able to identify our victim? Would his identity unlock the key to his murder? If so, hopefully it would help me solve the murder of Troy Gandy, because, as of right now, we didn't have a single viable suspect in his strangulation.

Within minutes, Cassandra paused the video and stabbed the monitor's screen with her index finger. "That's him."

I studied it and frowned, asked her to play it from when he first appeared in the camera. She rewound the tape and replayed it to show the man walking into the store. The camera at the entrance was the best angle to capture his face, but dark sunglasses and a red ball cap obscured most of his features.

"Do you have a better shot of his face?" I asked. "Maybe one without the sunglasses?"

Cassandra sped up the tape and we watched people come and go throughout the noon hour until our mystery man finally walked out, but it didn't show his face. She switched angles and views and played the footage around the times he arrived and left, but none of the angles offered a clear view of his face.

"Can you capture all of this footage and burn it to a disc for me?" I asked. "Even though I can't identify him, I'll still need it for evidence."

While she set out to download the footage, I leaned back in the chair and crossed my arms, thoughtful. "Did he tell you what he was looking for?" I finally asked.

"No, but he made me stop the tape when three boys walked up to the payphone and began playing with it." She shoved a blank DVD into the CD bay on her computer and waited for it to load. "He asked me to print out pictures of the boys and then he asked me if I knew who they were."

"Do you?"

She shook her head. "I think I've seen them in the store before, but I don't know who they are."

"Did you give him the pictures?"

"I did. They looked like high school kids, so I told him he might try going to Attakapas High School. Everyone in Mechant Loup goes to Attakapas High, so, unless they're from somewhere else, someone at the school should know who they are."

I watched idly as she pulled the video file up on the screen and began playing it to make sure it had copied correctly onto the DVD.

She stopped it at the part where the man was approaching the front door and she was about to eject the DVD when I sprang to my feet.

"Wait!" I said. "Play it again."

She jerked in her chair. "Jesus! You scared me."

I mumbled an apology and leaned closer to the monitor as she clicked on the video file and hit the *play* button. The man was seen ambling toward the front entrance and he was shoving a set of keys into his pocket. As he did so, the front of his shirt hiked up and I could see his belt buckle.

"Can you zoom in on his buckle?" I asked, holding my breath.

"Sure." Cassandra highlighted the section around his stomach and clicked the magnifying glass icon. Suddenly, his belt buckle popped up larger than life on the screen.

I shoved a finger toward the American flag belt buckle with the black shadow of a bear in the foreground. "That's my guy!"

CHAPTER 27

Since it was Saturday and the schools were closed, I spent the rest of the morning speaking to friends—they were few—and relatives of Troy Gandy, but no one had a clue what could've happened to him. As expected, his mom was a total wreck. I'd made contact with his dad, but the man didn't seem bothered much by his son's murder. That infuriated me, but I managed to keep a lid on my anger and get the information I needed from him, which was next to nothing.

Before grabbing lunch from a drive-through, I drove out to Attakapas High just in case there was some kind of afterschool function taking place, but the place was locked up tight. After wolfing down my burger and fries, I headed to the office to make some calls. Someone in Gatlinburg had to be missing a private investigator.

After speaking with someone from the Gatlinburg Police Department, I then called Sevierville PD, Pigeon Forge PD, and the Sevier County Sheriff's Department, but no one had filed any missing person reports for a private investigator.

When I hung up the phone after making the last call, it was nearing five o'clock and I was beginning to feel frustrated. That blue Nissan truck had to be somewhere close by. As far as I could tell from watching Mr. Pellegrin's video footage, it had never left Dire Lane. What if it was stashed away in someone's garage?

The thought brought me to my feet. I couldn't get a warrant for every garage down that street, but there was no law that prevented me from knocking on every door and asking everyone for permission to search their garage, just as I'd done with Rick Vincent. If they didn't have anything to hide, they shouldn't have a problem with allowing me to search.

So, that's exactly what I set out to do, and two hours later I was no closer to finding the truck than before my bright idea. Everyone who had been home had cooperated fully. Although I had already searched the Vincent's garage, I stopped by and asked Judith how Cindy was doing.

She frowned. "I didn't realize how much she liked that boy. I took her to a counselor yesterday and we have another session on Monday. She's really having a hard time."

I looked around, but didn't see her son. "Where's Burton?"

"He and his friends are in the canal." She chuckled. "They think they're junior detectives now, and that they're going to solve the case for you."

I didn't laugh. "If they do, tell them I'll buy them dinner every Friday night for a year."

When I left Dire Lane, I drove to the shelter, where Susan was sweeping the hardwood floors in the great room. She looked up and wiped dust from her face when I walked inside.

"Any luck?"

I shook my head and grabbed a dustpan to help out. As I knelt before her and placed it on the ground to scoop up the mess, I told her everything I'd done.

She stopped what she was doing and stared down at me. "The guy in the video is the *victim*?"

"Yep."

"He's a P.I.?"

"Yep."

"Huh." She rested her arm on top of the broom handle. Her hair was pulled back into a bandana and her sleeves were rolled up over her toned shoulders. "I can't believe no one's reported him missing yet."

"I'll check with the school on Monday to see if he showed up there," I said. "Maybe they'll have a good face shot of him from their cameras."

She shrugged and swept the trash into the dustpan and I walked it to the garbage can in the corner of the room.

"What about Jake Boudreaux?" I asked.

"He's still on the run. Sheriff Turner's got two deputies guarding Allie at the hospital and there's a car watching the grandparents' home where Sammy's staying."

After putting the dustpan on a nearby bookshelf, I walked over to Susan and wrapped my arms around her. We stared into each other's eyes for a long moment. She kissed me before turning her head and scanning our surroundings.

"I think it's ready." Her voice was laced with pride. "I stocked the pantry and refrigerator with food, the bathrooms are loaded with anything a woman might need for herself and her kids, and all of the beds are made. We're ready to roll."

I smiled warmly. Susan's vision—and tons of elbow grease—had turned this old dilapidated plantation home into a secure and charming refuge for battered women and their children. There were twelve bedrooms, seven bathrooms, two kitchens, a vast dining room, a great room, a sitting room, and a laundry room with three stacked washer and dryer sets.

"I'm sending out an email blast to the police social service divisions of all the neighboring parishes." She leaned her head into my chest. "And you know what I hope their response is?"

"What's that?" I asked.

"I hope they tell me I've done this for nothing, because there's no more violence against women and children."

CHAPTER 28

Sunday, October 2

Melvin was still at the police department when I walked in at seven o'clock Sunday morning. He greeted me with a smile and a slap on the back. "It's good to see you walking around here again."

I thanked him and asked why he hadn't gone home yet. "Didn't your shift end at six?"

"I'm waiting on a call from an informant who might know where Jake Boudreaux is hiding."

My ears perked up. "If you're going after him, I want in."

"Absolutely! It'll be like old times."

I went into my office and began the most boring but important part of police work—report writing. It took me a little over an hour to get the first draft of my report up to date and I was about to start working on the crime scene sketch when Melvin burst into my office.

"It's Jake—I know where he's at!"

I dropped my triangular architect scale ruler and chased him out the door, down the steps, and into the parking lot. I jumped into the front passenger side of his F-250 and, after snapping my seatbelt in place, held on for dear life.

"Where are we heading?" I asked.

"East Coconut Lane, last trailer on the left. He was just seen going in the back door."

I gritted my teeth as I stared out the window at the houses that blurred by. I remembered the joy in little Sammy's face when he found out he was going to get to eat a hamburger—I'd seen the same expression on Abigail's face many times during her short life.

Children were a gift from above and I couldn't understand how any parent could neglect their offspring or abuse them in any way. I secretly hoped Jake would resist arrest. If he did, I would—

I suddenly caught myself. What would I do if he resisted? Would I go too far...again? I shuddered and wondered if I was really prepared to do my job in a fair and just manner. The man in me wanted to beat the snot out of Jake Boudreaux, but the cop in me knew I'd have to exercise restraint and use only that force which is necessary to apprehend him. Who would win? Even as we were coasting down Coconut Lane on our approach to the trailer, I didn't have an answer...and it scared me.

Like any tactically sound cop, Melvin stopped several doors down and out of sight of the target location. We each slipped out of the truck and met behind it.

"Want to come up through the woods?" Melvin asked. "It's dense enough that he'll never see us and it'll be unexpected."

"It's your call," I said. "I'm only along for the ride." *And the ass-whipping,* I thought, again fantasizing about Jake resisting.

Melvin nodded and then led the way across a shallow ditch and into the greenery. He picked his way carefully through the woods, dodging trees, ducking under low-lying branches, and avoiding picker bushes. He finally angled back toward the street and then stopped when we reached the tree line. He pointed to a moldy white trailer with faded yellow trim that was perpendicular to the tree line. "That's the one."

The crank-up windows on our end of the trailer were partially open and appeared to be for the master bedroom. There was a window on the back side of the trailer that opened into the same room. The window frame and glass had been ripped out and there was only a rag covering the opening. Last I checked, rags couldn't keep out mosquitoes, so whoever lived there had to be miserable. I glanced down the back side of the trailer and saw a door, but it was padlocked from the outside. Unless they could walk through walls, no one was exiting from there.

"Can I have the front door?" Melvin asked. "So I can make contact with him?"

If Jake was going to be at the front door, that's where I wanted to be, but it wasn't my case. "This is your ballgame. I'll go wherever you tell me to go."

"Do you mind watching the back?" Melvin asked awkwardly. "I mean, only if you don't mind, Chief."

I smiled to reassure him. "I'm just here to help—and stop calling me Chief."

"Okay, Chief." Melvin took a deep breath and stepped slowly from behind the large maple where we'd been taking cover.

As he moved around the front of the trailer, I crouched low and made my way to the back corner near the busted-out window. I took up a position where I could watch the length of the back of the mobile home, as well as the end with the partially open crank-up windows.

All was quiet in the back, except for the wind blowing gently through the nearby trees. I moved my hand close to my pistol and waited for Melvin to knock on the door. I didn't have to wait long.

Immediately upon hearing a thunderous knock from the front of the trailer, heavy footsteps pounded from that side of the trailer and made their way toward the back, where I waited. A hollow-core door crashed open above me and the footsteps raced toward the busted-out window. I stood to my feet just in time to see a head and shoulders appear in the window. I recognized Jake Boudreaux's ugly face from the mugshot I'd seen earlier. He didn't see me as he grasped onto the outside of the trailer and pushed his right leg through the opening. There was a large kitchen knife in his right hand.

More footsteps sounded through the trailer as I stepped clear of the corner and drew my pistol. "Drop the knife or I'll shoot you right out of that window," I said in a calm and clear voice, hoping he wouldn't listen.

Jake's eyes grew wide and he let out an audible gulp. He immediately drew his leg back into the window and turned to retreat into the bedroom. I couldn't see into the room, so I didn't know who was barreling through and I didn't know if anyone was in danger. I was about to call out to Melvin when I heard him yell and then grunt. A bright flash emitted from the darkness of the room as a gunshot suddenly exploded inside. It was followed immediately by two more shots that were fired in rapid succession.

CHAPTER 29

"Melvin!" I sprinted around the trailer and rushed up the rocky steps. When I cleared the doorway, I hooked a right and rushed down the narrow hall. The door to the master bedroom was wide open and Melvin was squatting beside Jake, who was handcuffed and writhing in pain. The front of Jake's shirt was saturated in blood.

"I'm okay," Melvin said, looking up, "but he needs an ambulance."

I pointed to the front of Melvin's shirt, which was sliced vertically from the right side of his chest to his centerline. "Did he get you?"

Wiping sweat from his face, he shook his head and sprang to his feet. "My vest stopped it. I'm going get my first aid kit."

I pulled the police radio from my back pocket and turned up the volume. I then called dispatch and requested an ambulance at our location. Jake was cursing and complaining about how much it hurt, but I wasn't in the mood to hear it.

"Shut up and take your medicine like a man," I said, locating the knife on the ground a few inches from his body. Using my foot, I slid it away from him. Within seconds, Melvin appeared beside me and dropped to his knees to render first aid. While Melvin went to work, I squatted beside Jake and pushed his head back so he could see me.

"Do you think this is how Allie felt when you beat her with that pipe wrench?" I asked. "Do you?"

Jake stopped cursing for a brief moment to stare at me. I stared daggers back at him and he closed his eyes and turned away, groaning in pain. I watched Melvin and marveled at the effort he was putting into saving the man who had just tried to kill him. Melvin was as good as they came, that was for sure. Sighing heavily in resignation, I asked him if there was anything I could do to help out.

Melvin pointed to a hole in the shirt of Jake's lower torso that was leaking blood. "Can you apply pressure to that wound?"

I pulled a pair of latex gloves from Melvin's first aid kit and then opened a sterile pad. Applying more pressure than was necessary, I pushed the pad directly against the bullet hole in Jake's flesh. He winced in pain.

"Am I gonna die?" Jake asked in a display of pathetic cowardice. "It hurts so much!"

"No, you're going to be fine," Melvin said. "An ambulance is on the way."

"Tell them to hurry! It hurts so bad!"

I wanted to tell him to shut up, but sat quiet while Melvin continued consoling him. "I've always been told if you live long enough to know you've been shot, there's a good chance you'll survive," he said.

Jake looked over at Melvin, his face twisted in pain. "Really?"

"Yeah," Melvin said. "Really."

That seemed to calm Jake down a bit and it wasn't long before sirens screamed down the street and two medics rushed through the front door of the trailer. They each carried large toolboxes of lifesaving equipment, and I stepped back to make room for them to do their job. More steps sounded at the entrance to the trailer and I looked up to see Susan coming through the door. She wore her uniform, but her hair had been pulled back into a rough ponytail, and I knew she'd gotten dressed in a hurry.

With a single glance, she took in the scene.

"Melvin, are you okay?" she asked as one of the medics traded places with Melvin.

"Yes, ma'am. I'm fine." Melvin stood to his feet and slid by the medics and Jake.

Susan looked at me and I nodded. She sighed and grabbed her cell phone. "I'll call Sheriff Turner and ask if he can send a team down to work the shooting."

I nodded again and followed her out into the daylight. Melvin remained with the suspect and medics.

"What happened?" Susan asked after she finished speaking with Sheriff Turner.

I gave her the run down and she nodded.

"Thank God he was wearing his vest," she said.

"Yeah, he's lucky the bastard slashed at him rather than

stabbing."

"Mallory and Doug are on their way to work the case."

Mallory Tuttle was a solid detective, and Doug Cagle wasn't bad either.

I glanced at my watch. It wasn't even nine o'clock yet and we'd already managed to shoot someone. This was not how I'd wanted to start my day and, thanks to Jake Boudreaux, this was going to be a long one.

When the medics appeared at the front entrance to the trailer carrying Jake on a stretcher, Susan and I rushed forward to help them down the wobbly steps. They survived the descent and then loaded Jake into the back of the ambulance. He had been cuffed to the spine board.

Melvin tossed me the keys to his truck. "I'll ride to the hospital in the ambulance."

I nodded and stopped one of the medics before they walked to the cab. "What hospital are y'all taking him to?"

"Chateau General," he said.

"As soon as he's stable, can y'all get him out of there?" I asked. "He beat his wife severely with a pipe wrench and she's at Chateau General."

He nodded his understanding. "I'll make some calls. He's already stable, so we can transport him somewhere else."

I thanked him and turned to Susan. "I'll follow them to the hospital in Melvin's truck. That way, Mallory and Doug won't have to go far to find any of us."

"Okay. I'll secure the scene until they get here."

I started to walk off but Susan grabbed my hand. "I'm glad you're okay."

"Me, too," I said. "I've got too much work to do to be laid up again."

CHAPTER 30

Monday, October 3

Morning came early and I was in a sour mood when the alarm went off and disturbed my dreams. In my last dream, I was walking with my deceased daughter Abigail in a field filled with clovers, and she was trying to find one with four leaves. It felt so real that I was confused when I woke up and found myself sleeping beside Susan. She didn't even move and I touched her back to make sure she was breathing. Although we'd gotten home late last night because of the shooting investigation, Damian had worked her harder than ever. It was the first time I'd seen her so fatigued that she couldn't raise her hands to defend herself.

I slipped out of bed as quietly as I could and rushed through a shower. I got dressed, wrote a note on the bathroom mirror in soap telling Susan I loved her, and then rushed out the door. I hadn't even bothered to eat breakfast and I wasn't hungry. My mind was on one thing—identifying the private investigator in the morgue. With luck, the school would have something for me.

As I drove, I called Melvin to see how he was doing. Since he had worked the weekend shift, he was off for two days and should've been home enjoying his time off. Instead, he was at Chateau General Hospital.

"What're you doing there on your day off?" I asked. "Are you getting your shirt stitched up?"

He laughed. "Nope, I'm never getting that shirt fixed. I'm going to keep it as a reminder to always wear my vest."

Holding the steering wheel with my knee, I rubbed my chest

through my polo shirt. Maybe I should start wearing a vest, too, but it was so uncomfortable. I shrugged and asked him again what he was doing at the hospital.

"Claire and I picked up Sammy from his grandparents—they're elderly and don't get out much—and brought him to see Allie in the hospital."

Claire was Melvin's wife, and she was a good one. She loved that boy with all of her heart and it almost killed her when she walked into the hospital and saw the slash in Melvin's shirt. We had to peel her off the floor. Melvin was worried she might make another push for him to leave law enforcement, but she hadn't.

"That's nice of y'all," I said. "How's Sammy doing?"

"Great—all he does is talk about the police man with the gold badge who bought him a hamburger."

I smiled to myself as I ended the call and completed the twenty minute drive to Attakapas High School. When I checked into the office, a tall woman with blonde hair took my name and called the principal from her desk phone. After a brief conversation, she ushered me behind the counter, down a short hallway, and then pointed to an office. "Mr. Stew will be with you in a moment. Some student set off a stink bomb in the locker room and he's trying to get down to the bottom of it. He said you can make yourself at home in his office."

I nodded and sat in one of the wooden chairs in front of the desk. I didn't know the difference between simply waiting and making myself at home, so I just placed my file folder on the desk and sat there. I read the certificates on the wall while I waited. I read them twice. Every one of them.

I was about to head to the locker room to help solve the stink bomb mystery when a shadow appeared in the doorway. I turned to see a short man approaching. His stomach entered the room a full second before the rest of his body got there. While his gut was impressive, the rest of his body looked normal. Had he been pregnant, he would've been described as "all baby".

"Stewart Finane," said the man, extending a thin hand. After shaking, he sat behind the desk and sighed heavily. "Well, that was a mess. What can I do for you?"

I opened my file folder and fished out the still images I'd printed from the Mechant Groceries surveillance cameras. I selected one that showed the best view of our P.I. and slid it across the desk. "Do you remember this guy coming into the school a couple of weeks ago?"

Stewart pulled some reading glasses from the front pocket of his plaid shirt and shoved them high on his nose. Grabbing the photo, he squinted and studied it. "Is this that private investigator who was pretending to be a cop?"

"Could be. What do you know about him?"

He pushed his chair back and leaned toward the door. "Donna!" he yelled. "Can you come in here?"

The blonde lady appeared in the doorway almost immediately. "Yes, sir?"

Staring at her over the reading glasses, he waved Donna over. "Is this that guy who came in here pretending to be a cop?"

She stepped forward and studied the picture. She immediately nodded. "That's him." She turned to me. "He said he worked *with* law enforcement, to make it sound like he was a cop. But I wasn't fooled. I told him to have a seat and I called the sheriff's office. They never heard of him."

I caught my breath. "Do you remember his name?"

"No, but I have his business card." She turned to walk away, calling over her shoulder, "I'll get it real quick."

I was beaming on the inside. A name would open so many doors. I turned my attention to Principal Finane. "Why'd he come here?"

"As I recall, he was waving around some kind of wanted poster and he wanted my staff to identify it. When they told him they couldn't get involved, he asked to see a yearbook from the last three years." He shook his head. "They told him no and called for our school resource officer, but he left before the SRO got to the office."

"Did anyone see what he was driving?"

"Not that day, but he came back here the next day—that would've been Tuesday—and began stopping students as they left school grounds after band practice. One of our students, Kelli, said the man showed her a picture of Burton Vincent." He paused and took a breath. "And then on Wednesday, another student named Billy said a man fitting that description came back and identified himself as Burton's grandfather. Billy said the man claimed he was supposed to get Burton from school, but he was afraid Burton might've gotten on the bus already. Billy saw the man walk to a blue truck. He said it was an old one and it had a covered truck bed.

"By the time our SRO got out there he was gone. I had Donna contact Burton's parents to let them know what was going on." He shrugged. "We never saw him again."

That's because he was at the bottom of Westway Canal, I thought, nodding slowly. This was definitely my guy. "When did y'all call Burton's parents?"

Finane's brow furrowed. "I believe we called on both days—Tuesday when Kelli spoke to the man and again on Wednesday when he made contact with Billy."

"I'll need to interview Billy and Kelli."

"Right away." Stewart pulled out a chart and ran his finger down the page. He then picked up his handset and made two calls, asking teachers to send Billy and Kelli to the office. "They'll be here in a minute."

Just then, Donna returned carrying an old and faded business card. She handed it to me. "Here it is."

The card had soft perforated edges. It looked like one of those homemade jobs that were printed on the computer and then torn from the page. The writing was faint, but I turned it to the light and read the name out loud. "Fowler Underwood." I grunted. "F.U."

CHAPTER 31

Kelli didn't know much. While Principal Finane looked on, I questioned her about her encounter with Fowler Underwood. Apparently very shy, her face turned beet red every time I asked a question.

"All I remember was when I left band there was this undercover cop standing alongside the road and he showed me a picture," she said slowly, pulling at her dark hair as she spoke. "He asked me if I knew who it was and I told him it was Burton. He asked me if I knew Burton's last name and I told him."

"What made you think he was an undercover cop?" I asked.

"He showed me a badge and he said he worked with the police to find people."

"Did you tell Burton?"

She shook her head. "He's a football player. I don't really talk to them. They're all kind of loud, you know?"

"Did the man ask you any other questions?"

Kelli was thoughtful. She finally nodded. "He asked me if I knew where he lived and if I knew his mother. I told him no and then he asked if I knew what bus he rode."

"Did you?"

She shook her head.

"Did he ask any more questions?"

She shook her head again and I thanked her for her time. When Billy was seated beside me, I asked what he remembered about his encounter with Fowler Underwood.

"Is that his name?" He grunted. "Weird name. Yeah, this guy comes up to me right before school lets out as I'm taking down the

American flag. He says he's Burton's grandpa. He says he was there to pick up Burton but he was afraid Burton had already left on the bus."

"Had he?" I asked.

Billy shook his head. "Nah, the bell hadn't rung yet."

"Did you tell Mr. Underwood which bus Burton rode?"

"Yes, sir. I pointed to it and told him the bus was still there, so Burton was still there."

"You didn't tell me that when I questioned you," Principal Finane blurted. "Why not?"

Billy smirked. "You didn't ask."

"I understand from Principal Finane that you saw the man's truck," I said, not appreciating the interruption. "Do you remember what it looked like?"

"It was old and blue. It had one of those covers over the bed." He shrugged. "That's about it."

"What did the man do when he finished talking to you?"

"He went sit in that truck."

"Did you ever see him again?"

Billy cocked his head to the side. "I didn't see *him*, but I saw his truck leave as my bus was pulling out. Burton and I don't ride the same bus and I wasn't paying attention, so I don't know if he got in with his grandpa or not."

After I thanked him, Finane sent him back to class.

I sat there for a moment, pondering what I'd learned. It was clear Underwood thought there was something to this strange phone call he'd received from Mechant Loup. The wily old fellow had managed to track Burton to his high school and then had followed his bus home. But had he made contact with Burton on Wednesday? If he had, it hadn't been a long conversation, because he was seen leaving the street soon after he drove down it. He was back in the neighborhood for an hour on Thursday morning and then his truck disappeared back there on Friday morning.

"Can you check the attendance log for Burton Vincent for that Thursday and Friday?" I asked. "The twenty-second and twenty-third of September."

Finane buzzed Donna and asked her to find Burton's attendance record and bring it to him. Once he had it, he nodded. "Yep, Burton was here both days."

I stood and shook his hand. "I appreciate the time."

Once I was outside, I called Susan on the walk to my truck. It was another clear and beautiful day. While it had begun in the low sixties, the temperature had climbed into the mid-eighties already, and it was only ten o'clock.

Before I could tell Susan what I'd learned, she began speaking excitedly about how she'd offered to let Allie and Sammy stay in the shelter and Allie had agreed. "They're going to be our first guests!"

While I was happy for her, I was also a bit intimidated. I didn't know anything about running a shelter, and I said as much.

"You let me worry about that," she said. "You just solve this murder case so the town can go back to sleep. People are starting to whisper that we have a killer in our midst and it's starting to cause some of the townspeople to feel uneasy."

I scowled, not pleased with the progress of the case myself. I'd worked enough murders to know most of them weren't solved overnight, but I wanted to put this case to bed. I told her what I'd found out, and she asked me to relay the information to Mayor Cain.

"I spoke to Pauline this morning and she was asking how you were coming along." Susan paused. "I think she's worried you won't stay on."

I smiled and, although she couldn't see me, shook my head. "Not a chance. I'm happy to be back in the saddle."

"And I'm happy to hear it."

After making plans to meet up for lunch, we ended the call and I drove to the office. I couldn't wait to look up Fowler Underwood and find out what he was about. Now that I had a name, it would open all kinds of doors—it might even open the door to the suspect.

CHAPTER 32

Once I was in my office at the police department, I called Mayor Cain and let her know everything I'd learned up to that point. She was unbothered by the progress of the case, saying she was confident I would solve it in good time, but she asked me more than once how I liked the job and if I needed anything. She seemed satisfied once I told her how fulfilling it was to be doing police work again.

"I'm in it for the long haul," I said, "so you'd better not go losing any elections."

She promised to remain mayor as long as I agreed to continue working as the town detective.

As we spoke, I began a basic name inquiry on Fowler Underwood. By the time we'd ended the call, I was holding a printout and perusing the details. There wasn't much to the man. He was born on Memorial Day sixty-five years ago and he lived in Birchtown, Tennessee. I'd never heard of Birchtown, so I looked it up. It was a rural community in Blackshaw County and it was such a small town it didn't have its own police department.

I did an Internet search for private investigators named Fowler Underwood, but there were none. Next, I accessed the Tennessee database of private investigators and ran a name inquiry on Underwood. When the search results returned, I learned that there wasn't a Fowler Underwood with a P.I. license in any part of Tennessee. Maybe he'd let his license expire? What if he wasn't even a real private investigator? What if he was some sort of imposter? His business card did seem homemade.

"What the hell were you investigating, man?" I asked out loud, staring at his picture.

I thought about calling the Blackshaw County Sheriff's Department, but decided to map out the route instead. It was ten hours from the front door of the police department to Underwood's address. I needed to go up there and find some answers. It was possible the killer followed him down here and then returned to Tennessee, but that would mean Troy Gandy's murder was unrelated. I shook my head. The two cases had to be related. It was too coincidental.

I leaned back in my chair and threw my legs up on my desk to think. What if Troy was riding down Dire Lane when the killer was leaving in Underwood's old blue truck? The killer might've known the truck had been featured in the local news. If Troy saw the killer in the truck, he or she might feel compelled to get rid of Troy.

I needed to know what Underwood knew, and that meant I needed to get to his house or office. I had to view his records. But how would I get inside his house? And what if I was wrong about Underwood being in the morgue? What if he was still alive and was the actual killer?

I dropped my boots to the floor and conducted another inquiry, this time trying to find out if Underwood had any living relatives. It appeared his wife was deceased and he had two children; a girl named Melissa—if the information was correct—and a son who carried his name. The most recent address listed for Junior was at least five years old, and it was his dad's house. It appeared Melissa had fallen off the face of the earth. The last time she was listed at her dad's address, or any address, was eighteen years ago, and I couldn't find anything else under her name.

I called Susan to tell her I'd have to head to Tennessee.

"Tonight?" she asked.

"No…right now. I want to get there as soon as I can so I can be home by tomorrow."

"Does that mean you're standing me up for lunch?"

"I would never stand you up. I'll leave after we eat." I got on my cell phone as I walked out to the sidewalk and strode down the street to meet her. When the mayor answered, I let her know what I'd found out and told her I wanted to do some digging in Tennessee. "If I can find out what this Underwood fellow was working on, it might shed some light on my case."

She agreed it was the right thing to do and told me she'd have her secretary cut me a check for expenses.

"No time for that," I said. "I'm leaving as soon as I eat lunch with Susan."

"Keep your receipts," she said as I ended the call.

I wasn't worried about receipts. My mind was already in Tennessee, wondering what I'd find. Truth be told, I didn't even want to stop for lunch. I wanted to be there already.

CHAPTER 33

1:38 p.m.
Chateau General Hospital

After Clint left for Tennessee, Susan had contacted the jail to make sure Jake Boudreaux was still locked up. Once she'd received confirmation that he was, she'd picked up Sammy and headed to the hospital.

"How're you feeling?" Susan asked Allie, who was gingerly slipping on her sandals.

Allie clutched at her side with one hand and straightened over the crutches once her sandals were strapped in place. "It still hurts, but at least I can move around now."

Sammy stood near Allie and his face was scrunched up as he watched his mom. "Mommy, do you want me to carry you?"

Susan and Allie laughed, but Allie stopped abruptly. "It hurts to laugh." Balancing on the crutches, she patted Sammy's head. "No, my little tiger…Mommy can walk."

A nurse walked in with the discharge papers and handed them to Allie. "Okay, you're free to leave. I already went over your home care instructions, but they're written on this form in case you forget."

Allie took the forms and tucked them under her arm while Susan gathered up her bags of clothes.

"What about all of the stuff I have at home?" Allie asked. "Everything I own is in that house."

"We'll stop by and get as much of your personal items as possible," Susan promised. "After the trial and once we find you a permanent residence, we'll help you get everything out."

"What if Jake gets out of jail first and destroys all my stuff?"

Susan waved her hand. "He's not getting out. His bond's half a million dollars. And even if he did post bail, the detention center would notify us in advance and we'd be able to get a U-haul truck out there and pick up everything before he gets back home."

"Good. I hope he rots in jail." She patted Sammy's head. "Are you ready to move into our new temporary home?"

"What about my toys?" he asked. "Will I get to play with them again?"

"Once we stop at the house, you can pick out five of your favorite ones to bring with us," Allie said. That seemed to satisfy Sammy and he strolled along beside Allie.

Susan followed them down the hall. She was smiling on the inside. This was what she'd always wanted to do—help women get out of abusive relationships—and, thanks to Clint and a few unfortunate circumstances, she was realizing that dream.

Once everyone had piled into Susan's Tahoe, she paused to check her phone, hoping Clint had contacted her. She frowned when he hadn't. This would be her first night apart from him since they'd moved in together, and it made her a little sad.

After a quick stop at Allie's house for more clothes and Sammy's toys, Susan drove them to the shelter at the end of Paradise Place.

"Do you live in the house at the beginning of the street?" Allie asked, pointing to it when they passed.

Susan nodded. "If you need anything at all, just give me a call. All of my contact information is written on the peg board in the kitchen."

Susan and Clint had talked about installing a gate at the entrance to Paradise Place, and she made a mental note to get working on it. It would be another layer of security and it wouldn't hurt.

"Wow! It's so big!" Sammy said when he stepped out the back of the Tahoe and stared up at the old plantation home. "Is this our new house, Mommy?"

"No, sweetie, we're just staying here for a little bit until it's safe to go back home."

"I want to stay forever!" Sammy ran over and lumbered up the steps and onto the porch. He ran back and forth along the length of the porch, laughing at the sounds his shoes made on the hollow wood.

Susan smiled. "He's precious."

"He's the best thing that ever happened to me."

"Clint thinks he's awesome." The corner of Susan's mouth curled downward, thoughtfully. "I saw the way Clint looked at him, as though he wished for a child again."

"What do you mean, *again*?"

Susan told Allie what had happened with Abigail, watching as Allie's eyes widened in horror.

"Dear Lord, that's horrible!" Allie said.

Susan nodded. "He doesn't talk about it much, but I can still see the pain in his eyes sometimes. It's like he's looking at me but not even seeing me. And then he'll snap out of it and get embarrassed for not hearing what I was saying."

"I bet he was an amazing father. He was so good with Sammy…unlike that piece of shit, Jake." Tears formed in Allie's eyes. "The sad thing is that Sammy loves his dad so much. He doesn't know what a bad man he is and I'm afraid it'll break his little heart when he realizes he won't be seeing Jake anymore."

"Let's not dwell on that now." Susan said, putting a hand around Allie's back and helping guide her up the steps. "Let's just focus on getting you better."

Allie nodded and did her best not to lose her balance. "It's so hard to walk on crutches. I feel like such a spaz with these things."

Susan nodded her understanding and let go of Allie when she made it to the landing. She then unloaded all of their things and placed them in the room Allie had selected. When they were done in there, Susan showed her around the rest of the first level of the shelter. "I'll show you the upstairs once your leg is healed."

"I appreciate that," Allie said. "I had a hard enough time making it up the steps. I couldn't imagine going way up there."

"Well," Susan said after a bit, "I have to get back to work. Call if you need anything."

She ambled back to her Tahoe and stopped to check her email account from her phone. She'd received messages from half a dozen police social service officers congratulating and thanking her for what she was doing. She smiled and tossed her phone on the console. The sense of accomplishment she felt was like none other. "When I die," she said aloud to no one, "I want to be remembered for helping women and children in need."

As though in response to her statement, the police radio scratched to life and Lindsey's voice boomed through the speakers. Susan jerked at the unexpected noise and laughed at herself, but stopped suddenly when Lindsey told Takecia to respond to North Project Road.

"A farmer located a blue truck on the property," Lindsey said.

"He thinks it's the one from the news."

Susan fired up her engine and smashed the accelerator, racing up Paradise Place and then north on Main. Without taking her eyes off the road, she grabbed her phone and called Clint. He answered on the first ring.

"Where are you?" she asked, glancing at the clock on the dash. Clint had left at twelve-thirty and it was now a little after two.

"Just getting into Mississippi." Clint must've had his radio on, because he asked if she was heading to North Project Road.

"Yeah, I'm just down the highway. Do you want me to process it, or wait until you get back?" she asked.

Clint hesitated. "Do you think I should come back? I can make this trip later in the week."

"No," Susan said quickly. "You have to find out what Underwood was investigating. I'll process the area where the truck was located and then secure it in the sally port. I can work it up if you like, or I can just lock it down for when you get back."

"No, you can work it if you want. I wonder how long it's been back there."

"It couldn't have been before Wednesday, because we would've seen it on the tape from Mr. Pellegrin."

"That's true." Clint hesitated again, then finally sighed. "Okay, just be careful. We don't know who the killer is and—"

"And what? Are you worried about me?"

"I'm always worried about you."

"That's so flattering"—Susan slowed as she approached the intersection to North Project Road—"but you don't need to worry about me. You need to worry about whoever crosses me."

Clint chuckled. "Still, be careful."

"I will." The phone bounced against her ear as the Tahoe jostled over the uneven surface. She saw a tractor on the northern shoulder of the road just ahead and she told Clint she'd have to go. "I'm pulling up to the farmer who called it in, so I've got to get out."

"Let me know what you find…and be safe."

She hung up and saw movement in her rearview mirror. Squinting to see through the cloud of dust she'd left in her wake, she recognized Takecia's patrol cruiser flying up behind her.

CHAPTER 34

The farmer was an old wiry guy with a bent back. He had to lean to the side and push his straw hat high on his head to look up at Susan. Lindsey had told Susan his name was Chet Robichaux, which meant he was related to half the townspeople, as Robichaux was a common name in these parts.

"How are you, Mr. Robichaux?" Susan smiled warmly at the old man. "I bet you've had better days."

"Chief," he said simply, nodding his head in greeting and his agreement.

Susan glanced at the farm tractor with the large bush hog attached to the back of it. A wide path had been cut right down the middle of the field and it disappeared in the tall grass to the right. "Where'd you find the truck?"

He pointed northward across the field. "Somebody drove it right across the field and crashed it into the canal that borders our property to the right. I almost didn't see it."

Takecia walked up to Susan. "Chief, do you want me out here or you want me watching the town? There are two calls pending—a civil dispute and a lock-job."

"Yeah, handle those two complaints. I've got this." Susan turned back to Mr. Robichaux. "Can I drive my Tahoe across the field?"

He nodded. "It's bone dry. We haven't had rain in weeks. Follow me."

The old man climbed up on the tractor and fired it up. With the bush hog suspended in the air, he lumbered across the field and Susan followed him. They traveled along the path Robichaux had cut through the field, and the surrounding weeds swallowed them up.

They made a left through the maze of thick grass and then veered slightly toward the right. After traveling about two hundred yards, the mower path reached the very edge of the canal and Mr. Robichaux stopped his tractor.

Susan craned her neck to see over the grass that grew at the edge of the canal as she dismounted, but it wasn't until she walked around the front of her Tahoe that she saw taillights peeking up out of the thick weeds. She could see the back of the truck well enough to notice the license plate had been removed.

She squatted and studied the ground directly behind the truck where Mr. Robichaux had already passed the bush hog. It was so dry and packed that there wasn't even a hint of a trail. She looked toward the tall weeds from which the truck must have travelled, but she couldn't discern a pathway.

"You mind if I keep cutting?" the old man asked. "I've got to get this field cleaned before the sun goes down."

Standing to her feet, Susan nodded and thanked him for his time. She then drew her expandable baton and shook it out. She whacked at the weeds along the edge of the canal and cleared a path to the driver's door. Once she was beside it, she pulled some latex gloves from her shirt pocket and reached up to carefully open the door.

The ditch was deep and she had to push off of the front tire to climb into the cab. Once there, she pulled out her flashlight and shined it around the interior. It was empty. There wasn't a piece of paper or a receipt or any other item in the cab. It had been cleaned out. The windshield on the driver's side had been busted, but there wasn't any glass on the hood, which made it look like an old break. She slid her hand toward the crack in the dashboard where the VIN plate would be, but felt a mangled mess of metal and plastic.

"What the hell?" Retrieving her phone, she stretched out her arm and took a picture of the area. She then studied the image—it had been ripped out. "Someone doesn't want us to know who this truck belongs to."

Pushing against the steering wheel with her left hand, she crawled across the front seat and opened the glove box. It was empty. She pulled down the visors, checked the cracks in the seat, maneuvered her way to the narrow back area, and checked under the seats. Nothing.

After working her way out of the cab, she scrambled up the bank of the canal and lifted the back hatch of the camper shell and, taking a deep breath and holding it, slid belly-down into the bed of the truck. It was also empty.

After dropping back to the ground, she made a thorough search of the area surrounding the truck and began taking photographs, but she was unable to locate anything of evidentiary value. Everything was so dry that the person who crashed the truck had been able to walk away without leaving a trace.

Wiping sweat from her forehead, Susan called Lindsey and asked her to have a wrecker proceed to her location. A cool breeze began to blow and it felt good against her skin. She was shoving her radio into her belt clip when the rustling weeds parted for a split second and sunlight glinted off of something deep in the canal. It was off to the right of the truck, about forty feet away.

Susan walked along the canal—pushing thick clumps of weeds down with her boots as she proceeded forward—and curiosity mounted as more sunlight flickered through the foliage. When she was standing directly over the object, she took a careful step into the canal and pushed some of the heavier bushes to the side. When it came into view, she grunted. It was a black and silver bicycle—Troy's bike.

"The same person who killed Fowler Underwood definitely killed Troy Gandy," Susan told Clint when he answered her call.

"How do you know that?" Clint asked.

"The killer dumped Troy's bicycle forty feet from where Fowler's truck was crashed in the canal."

"So, it's not a coincidence."

"I'm afraid not." Susan slid the rest of the way to the bottom of the canal, but managed to stay upright. She gave Clint a detailed description of the bicycle as she visually examined it. She pushed more weeds down with her foot when she saw something silver against the ground. She sat on her heels and moved the individual blades of grass aside. "Damn, this might be the murder weapon."

"What might be the murder weapon?" She could tell she had Clint's full attention. "What'd you find?"

"It's a three-foot piece of quarter-inch wire with a loop on each end." She leaned closer. "There're tiny pieces of flesh between the strands of wire, so it's definitely the murder weapon. And there's a padlock on one end of the wire. Troy used this to lock up his bicycle."

"The key from his pocket," Clint said. "I bet it opens the lock."

Although Susan knew Clint couldn't see her, she nodded, but it wasn't in response to his comment because she hadn't been paying attention to him. An idea had begun to form in her mind and it was growing stronger. "Troy rode up on something," she said slowly. "He wasn't targeted—he was at the wrong place at the wrong time."

"I think you're right," Clint said. "The padlock and wire combination was a weapon of opportunity. The killer took it from his bike and used it against him."

"We just need to figure out where he was when he was killed and what he stumbled into," Susan said. "One thing we do know—it was somewhere between his window and Cindy Vincent's back yard."

CHAPTER 35

6:13 a.m., Tuesday, October 4
210 Devil's Stretch, Birchtown, Tennessee

I pulled to the right-hand shoulder of the road and shut off my engine. The sun hadn't risen yet and it was dark, which made it hard to read the numbers on the houses I'd driven by. If my map was correct, that was Fowler Underwood's address up ahead to the north.

Devil's Stretch was a narrow mountain road that zigzagged sharply through Birchtown and northward into the mountains. There were no hotels in town, so I'd been forced to stay at a hotel twenty miles away in Gatlinburg. In Louisiana, twenty miles usually meant a twenty-minute drive, but not so in the mountains. It took me nearly forty minutes to get back to Gatlinburg. I hadn't gotten a room until a little after midnight, and I couldn't find an open place to eat, so I headed straight for bed. After a few restless hours of sleep, I'd taken a quick shower, packed up my stuff, skipped breakfast, and headed straight for Birchtown.

Although I'd skipped two meals, I wasn't hungry. All of my attention was on the yellow house that squatted between Devil's Stretch and the side of a mountain that seemed to extend way up into the Heavens. An orange Jeep with a ragtop was parked on the far right side of the gravel driveway, apparently making room for another vehicle that was absent. Could it be that the blue Nissan King Cab normally took up the space beside the Jeep?

I hadn't seen a car all morning and there wasn't a single light on in the house. After waiting a few more minutes, I stepped out of my Tahoe. It was sixty degrees outside and a cool wind was blowing in from the north. I shuddered as I started walking toward the house, wishing I'd brought a light jacket. With luck, Fowler, Jr. would be home and he could provide some answers.

My boots crunched in the gravel and I slowed my pace to minimize the noise. If he was inside, I didn't want him to know I was here until I was ready for him to know it. I ambled toward the mailbox and looked both ways along Devil's Stretch before opening the flap. The box was so full that several envelopes had been shoved forcefully inside, causing them to become crumpled.

I scanned my surroundings again before removing one of the envelopes and straightening it against the side of the box. I then pulled out my phone, shined the light on it, and read the caption out loud, "Fowler Underwood, Two-One-Zero Devil's Stretch, Birchtown, Tennessee." I shoved the mail back into the box and walked directly to the back door. Either no one was home or Fowler's son was too lazy to even catch the mail.

I tried calling Susan, but the call failed. I tried a few more times after walking around a bit, but I couldn't get service. I used the camera on my phone and took a picture of the license plate on the Jeep. I'd call later and have Susan run it just to be sure it was registered to one of the Underwoods.

I then walked to the back door and banged on it. There was no movement from inside. I banged a second time—this time harder—but it brought no response from inside. I then tried the door handle, but it was locked. I walked around to the front of the house, where a wooden picket fence was wrapped around the entire front yard.

There were no gates, so I jumped over the fence and walked across the wooden porch. I banged on the back frame and tried the knob, but no one came to the door and it was locked. I had hoped to find someone who could answer some questions.

I hurried back to my Tahoe and drove until I reached the fork in the road where Birchtown Creek Baptist Church was located. The nearest neighbor was a short drive to the right, but I saw a car in the parking lot of the church. It hadn't been there when I'd passed earlier, so I pulled in and tried the door knob. Like all good churches, it was open and I stepped inside to find a preacher standing at the lectern. His head was down, but he looked up when my boots sounded on the hollow floor.

"Welcome to Birchtown Creek Baptist Church," he greeted warmly in his mountain twang. "What can I do you for?"

I introduced myself and told him I was looking for anyone related to Fowler Underwood. "I need to speak with his nearest relative," I said. "It's a matter of great importance."

"Well, that's troubling news." The preacher shifted the large-rimmed glasses on his nose. "Since you're looking for his next of kin, I can only guess he's either dead or in a bad way."

I frowned. "He's definitely not well."

"As far as I'm aware, the only remaining relative is a son— Fowler, Jr.—but he's been jailed for six months up at county. He's awaiting trial on drug charges and also doing time for not paying his child support." He paused and shook his head. "Junior gave his dad a fair amount of grief, that's for certain."

"What do you know about Fowler Underwood?"

"I know just about all of it—same as everyone around these parts. Fowler was born an only child, married young, had a daughter and a son, raised them the best he could, and then tragedy struck." The preacher slid a thin ribbon book marker between the pages of the Bible and folded it shut. He then walked around the lectern and pointed to one of the pews.

I took a seat and he sat a few feet from me, on the same pew.

"It was eighteen years ago, right down yonder." The preacher nodded his head farther north of where we were. "Fowler had purchased this little stretch of land and put a trailer on it for his daughter, Melissa. She hadn't been there a month when it happened."

He paused and shook his head slowly as he removed his glasses and wiped them carefully with a handkerchief he had pulled from his shirt pocket. When he was done, he shoved them back on his face and continued. "Her husband, Larry Cooper, was a little pecker-head from town. Fowler was convinced the only reason Melissa married Cooper was because he'd gotten her pregnant. But, while Fowler didn't like the boy, he was determined to see his girl happy, so he bought them a little place to raise his grandchild."

The preacher paused again and I nearly groaned out loud. I wanted to reach down his throat and drag the information out, but, instead, I sat patiently and let him tell it in his own time.

"There's a lot of speculation surrounding what happened that night and who done it, but one thing they know for sure—Larry Cooper was gunned down and Melissa and her baby boy was gone. They never seen hide nor hair of that girl or her child again." The preacher shook his head. "It 'bout killed poor Fowler when he walked in that trailer and found Larry dead and his girl missing."

That got my attention and I felt bad for the man. "Fowler's the one who discovered the crime?"

The preacher nodded. "And like I said, it 'bout killed him.

Eventually, it did kill his wife, Lord bless her soul, but not before she put up a good fight trying to find Melissa."

"What agency handled the case?"

"I don't know if you can call it *handled*, it's more like *mishandled*. Fowler was outspoken about the investigation and criticized Sheriff Burns of Blackshaw County to everyone who would listen. He believed Burns was either involved in a cover-up or he was simply incompetent. He tried calling in the state police to make Burns drop the warrant on his daughter, but they refused to get involved, saying they wouldn't interfere with a local matter. They said the only way they'd step in was if the sheriff requested their assistance, and he certainly wasn't going to do that."

"Is Sheriff Burns still in power today?" I asked.

The preacher shook his head. "He's long gone—booted out of office. Fowler raised so much hell and caused so much trouble for him that he couldn't take it anymore. One day, he just up and punched Fowler on a busy sidewalk in the middle of town. Knocked him right out. When Fowler hit the ground, Burns began stomping him until a few of the townspeople dragged him away. He resigned the next day."

"Why'd Fowler criticize the sheriff and the investigation?"

"Because Burns immediately named Melissa as a suspect in Larry's murder and he swore out a warrant for her. Fowler insisted his daughter was in danger and he continues to believe that until today…" The preacher allowed his voice to trail off as he glanced up at me. "Well, he continues to believe that to this day if, indeed, he's still with us today. Your presence here makes me doubt that he is."

I frowned, shook my head. "Fowler was murdered in our parish two Fridays ago."

The preacher recoiled in horror. "Murdered? Who would want to kill old Fowler? He's never said a bad word to no one except Sheriff Burns, and most folks around these parts felt it was justified."

"That's why I'm here, to try and find out who killed him." After providing the details of the case that had already been made public, I asked about Fowler. "You said he raised hell and caused trouble for Burns. What exactly did he do?"

"For starters, when the sheriff circulated wanted posters around town naming Melissa as the suspect in Larry's murder, Fowler went behind him and tore them all down. Burns arrested him for tampering with evidence, but the DA refused to accept the charges. He later began showing up at town hall meetings and demanding that Burns tender his resignation. After Burns attacked him, he finally let it go."

The preacher scowled. "He missed his daughter and grandbaby so much that he hired some forensic artists from up at the college to make some age progression portraits of Melissa and her baby so he could see what they looked like today. He'd heard about the technology on the news. People who had lost kids at an early age would have the pictures done so they would know what their kids looked like as adults, and he did the same thing."

"Did those portraits end up on a flyer?"

The preacher nodded. "Last year, on the anniversary of Melissa's disappearance, one of Fowler's sisters-in-law—Melissa's nanny—made up about a thousand flyers with those pictures and put them up all around the eastern part of the state. They were making one last-ditch effort to bring Melissa home before Fowler grew old and passed away. I know he never gave up on Melissa and he missed her and his grandbaby more than anything in the world."

"What's the anniversary date of their disappearance?"

"The Fourth of July."

I was suddenly angry at Kegan Davis. The little punk had made a conscious decision to prank call a victim's family and lie about knowing where they were. Not only was it a cruel joke to a grieving father, but, thanks to his harassing phone call, poor Fowler Underwood was now dead, and so was Troy Gandy.

"Do you know the baby's name?" I asked.

The preacher's brow furrowed. "If I remember correctly, it was Drake…Drake Cooper. I baptized him when he was just a couple of months old."

I jotted down the information and sat thoughtful, wondering where to go from here. "Does Junior know anything?"

"No, he was twelve at the time so he didn't know much, but it did have an impact on his life. Fowler and his wife were so tore up over losing Melissa that they neglected him a bit." The preacher removed his glasses again and rubbed his face. "That's most likely why he turned out the way he did."

"Where can I find Sheriff Burns?" I was beginning to wonder if he had made the trip to Louisiana and killed Fowler.

"Why do you want to talk to him?" the preacher asked.

"He investigated the case, so he knows more about it than anyone else."

"If you say so. He lives five miles south of Birchtown, down a dirt road off to the right." He shook his head. "I wouldn't drive down that road without being invited. Word is he's gotten a little crazy in his old age and he's prone to shooting at trespassers."

"Thanks." I stood to leave. "I'll take my chances."

CHAPTER 36

The dirt road was right where the preacher said it would be, but he'd failed to mention how overgrown the road was. Old hickory trees grew unfettered, their low-lying branches scraping the top of my SUV as I drove along the bumpy road. I winced at the sounds the branches made overhead, wondering if I'd need a new paintjob after I was done.

My headlights popped on automatically as I crept into the deep mountain shadows. The road switched right and angled steeply upward, forcing me to drop it into low gear. After negotiating several more switchbacks, the ground leveled off and I saw a structure up ahead. Remembering what the preacher had said, I pulled my Tahoe to a stop, shut off the engine, and stepped out.

"Sheriff Burns!" I yelled loudly, slowly approaching what I could now see was a rustic log cabin. I kept my hands out to my sides to show I was not going to reach for a gun. I wasn't wearing a holster, but my Beretta 9mm pistol was tucked into the waistband under my shirt. "Sheriff Burns, I'm Clint Wolf from Louisiana—"

I shut up and stopped dead when I heard the unmistakable sound of a pump-action shotgun being racked. It echoed sharply through the quiet mountain air.

"What the hell do you want, Clint Wolf from Louisiana, and who told you where to find me?" His voice sounded hoarse and raspy, like a heavy smoker and drinker.

"I'm a fellow law enforcement officer," I said calmly. "Here to talk about a case you worked years ago. I need your help."

"Bullshit! You're some kind of fed, aren't you? Well, if it's my guns you want, come and get 'em!"

I laughed out loud.

"What the hell is so funny?"

"What's funny is you thinking I'm after your guns," I said. "If anyone came after your guns, I'd be standing shoulder to shoulder with you."

Suddenly, Sheriff Burns materialized from behind a tree as smoothly as I've often seen fog moving through the swamps back home. Bushy brows hovered over black eyes and the bottom portion of his face was covered in a thick black and white mop of a beard.

"Turn your back to me and pull out your credentials—slowly! And if you go for that pistol you've got hidden under your shirt, I'll cut you in half!"

Burns was probably sixty, but he looked strong as a mule and mean as a rattler. His loose-fitting, long-sleeved khaki shirt was tucked into his rugged khaki pants and there was a pistol snapped into a leather holster on his right side. His pants were held up with a belt that boasted an American flag buckle with the shadow of a bear in the foreground—*must be popular around here*—and there was no doubt in my mind he would use the shotgun in his hands if he felt it necessary.

Following his orders, I carefully turned, removed my wallet from my back pocket, and then stood there holding it above my head in my left hand.

"Now throw it back over your head in the direction of my voice."

I tossed it toward him and waited, trying not to lose my patience with him. I needed him to talk to me, so I would jump through as many hoops as he required. I couldn't afford to piss him off.

The next time he spoke, his voice boomed in my ear and it startled me a little. I hadn't even heard him pick up my wallet and here he was right behind me.

"You can take your wallet back. You're no fed."

"I could've told you that." I took my wallet from his hand and shoved it back in my pocket.

Throwing the shotgun over his shoulder, he fixed his suspicious eyes on me and adjusted the wide-brimmed leather hat on his head. "What case are you here about? I ain't been sheriff in over fifteen years."

"I'm here about Melissa Cooper."

"That case?" I saw his shoulders droop a little, but his expression was unwavering. "What about it?"

"I'd like to hear your take on it. I'm especially interested in what you found at the crime scene."

"Why would a cop from Louisiana"—he pronounced it Loo-zee-ana—"be interested in a case that happened in Blackshaw, Tennessee eighteen years ago?"

"It might be connected to a murder case I'm working."

He grunted. "Oh, yeah? Who was murdered?"

"Fowler Underwood."

That brought a reaction from the old timer. His eyebrows arched upward a bit and he licked his lips. "I see. Well, come on up to the house."

Burns turned and headed up a steep rocky driveway, with me on his heels. I followed him up his front steps, which were made of split logs, and onto the solid wood porch. He lifted a latch and pushed open the door, which was made of thick planks but seemed wobbly on its hinges, as though it could be pushed open with ease. There were cracks in the chink between some of the logs and when I stepped inside I could see light bleeding through.

I pointed to one of the cracks. "How do you keep the mosquitoes out?"

"We don't have mosquitoes out here." He moved across the tiny room, which was a living room/kitchen combination, and grabbed a black kettle and a coffee cup. "Care for some java?"

"I rarely touch the stuff."

He let out a grunt of disapproval and settled into a homemade wooden chair that had a bear hide stretched over it. He pointed to a matching chair. "I don't get much company up here, so excuse the order of the place."

"Not a problem," I said, watching him loosen the red bandana that was tied around his throat. His hands were rough and cracked. They were even bleeding in a couple of places. I pointed to the pistol in his holster. "Model 1911—is it a Browning?"

"Is there any other 1911?"

I turned up my hand, acknowledging his point. Realizing there would be no need for small talk and establishing a rapport—he would either tell me what I wanted to know or not—I just jumped right in. "What can you tell me about the incident involving Melissa Underwood Cooper?"

He studied me for a long moment, and then finally let out a growl and stood to his feet. He walked to a back room, which I figured was the only bedroom in the place, and I could hear some rustling noises and something fell to the floor. He cursed a bit, there was more movement, and then he mumbled something I couldn't decipher. When he reappeared, he was carrying a single piece of paper—it was the same kind of flyer Burton had described.

I took it from him and then looked up. "What about it?"

"I found that floating around town a few weeks ago. As far as I can tell, they're still missing and they've never been found. I'm afraid old man Underwood was right—his daughter was in danger and she met with her demise somewhere out there in the world."

"So, you don't think she murdered Larry Cooper anymore?"

He sighed. "It wouldn't be the only mistake I've made in my years."

"I was hoping you could tell me what you found at the scene."

"Son, I'm old and tired. Do you know how many cases I've worked in my career? Without the report in front of me, I'm afraid I can't answer your questions. The only independent recall I have is that Fowler Underwood was a pain in my ass, and I'm not too sorry to hear he's gone."

"That's not a nice thing to say," I mumbled, feeling disheartened by this turn of events. I'd originally figured he'd be happy to help me solve an old case, but I was smart enough to know that some investigators didn't appreciate Monday-morning quarterbacking. If he couldn't solve the case, I guess he figured no one could, and he didn't appreciate new blood coming along and second-guessing his actions. I decided to try once more. "Didn't you keep copies of your reports?"

He shook his head. "All of that stuff stayed at the sheriff's department."

"Don't you remember anything at all about the scene?"

"Anything I'd say would be guesswork, and you know we're not supposed to guess at such things."

I asked question after question, verbally attacking him from several different angles, but got nowhere. The man was a steel trap and wouldn't provide the slightest amount of information. I finally thanked him and left.

CHAPTER 37

After leaving Sheriff Burns' cabin, I drove around until I found a gas station. A young kid pumping gas was nice enough to give me the directions to the sheriff's department, and forty minutes later I was seated in a small office watching a man who was even older than Burns walk in carrying a cardboard box that had seen better days. It was ripped on one side and some pages were sticking out of the bottom. The old timer, a detective named Yates, dropped the box at my feet. "This is everything we've got on the Cooper killing."

I removed the flimsy lid and placed it on the floor beside the box. The first file in the box was labeled "Investigative Report". I pulled it out and flipped through the lower half of the report until I came to the last page, where I found Sheriff Burns' signature. The report was 126 pages long. I'd encountered cases that were mishandled before, and in almost all of those cases the one glaring common denominator was a lack of paperwork, which pointed to improper documentation.

"It sure is weird seeing this file again," the detective said. "I remember this case like it was yesterday. It's not too often we get a missing woman and baby under mysterious circumstances."

I nodded absently, thumbing through the report. I had learned early in my career that proper documentation was crucial to any case, and if this report was any indication of the efforts that had gone into the investigation, I'd say it was handled properly. I held up the report and glanced back up at Yates. "Did Sheriff Burns write this report himself, or did one of his detectives do it?"

"He wrote every word. Each time he'd get a new lead or some crack-head would confess to the murder, he'd follow up on it himself and add a supplemental report to the file. He was determined to see this case through to the end, even if it killed him."

I looked at the heading of the report. The call had come in at eleven-forty-eight at night; right after Fowler had gone to the trailer to see if they wanted some barbecue.

"I knocked on the door," Fowler said in his transcribed statement, *"but they didn't answer. I figured they couldn't hear me because of the fireworks going off, so I opened the front door. That's when I saw him on the sofa, shot full of holes."*

"Saw who?" asked Sheriff Burns.

"My son-in-law, damnit—I saw my son-in-law dead on the sofa, shot full of holes. Now, where the hell's my daughter?"

"I've got a team of investigators out there looking for her," Burns had said. *"As for now, I need you to tell me exactly what you saw and heard from the time you left your house to the time you found Larry."*

"I already told you everything."

"I heard Sheriff Burns put a beating on Fowler Underwood," I said after reading in silence for a bit. "I heard it's what cost him his position."

Yates took a deep breath and exhaled. "That wasn't his finest moment. He had tried to be patient, tried to understand the pain Mr. Underwood felt, but the man's behavior finally got to him. Sheriff Burns was putting in countless hours on the case, running down every lead that came in, but every time he'd put up his flyers, Underwood would come behind him and tear them down. That didn't make the sheriff happy." He scowled. "Underwood was intentionally impeding the investigation into the case, and the sheriff began to think he had something to do with killing Larry and then helping his daughter get away."

I continued reading the report. According to the scene reconstruction, six rounds had been fired. Larry had been hit five times. One of the bullets had traveled above his head and through the thin trailer wall behind him. Other than Larry's dead body, there was no other evidence of injured persons in the trailer.

"So, what do y'all think happened to Melissa and the baby?" I asked.

"The sheriff thought Underwood helped them get away," Yates said simply. "He firmly believes Melissa killed Larry and he still thinks she's running from the law—even today. We did consider other possibilities, such as someone else killed Larry and Melissa managed to escape with her baby, but that seemed unlikely."

"What about you? Do you still think she's out there somewhere?

Running?"

"Absolutely." Yates sat on the corner of the desk and rubbed his white hair. "She's in the NCIC database, so if she would've been found anywhere in the country—either dead or alive—we would've known about it, so she has to be out there hiding."

I flipped to the next page of the report and whistled. *This is interesting!*

CHAPTER 38

"I see y'all recovered fifty thousand dollars worth of heroin in a gym bag under Larry's body on the sofa," I said. "Couldn't the murder have been drug-related?"

Yates leaned over to tap the report. "We recovered what we *thought* was heroin. Spoiler alert; when you get to page twenty you'll see that we performed a presumptive test on the drugs. Turns out it was bunk."

"Wait, are you saying he'd been selling counterfeit drugs to people? That's motive for murder if I ever heard one."

"No," he said. "Larry never had a chance to sell an ounce of it. When the sheriff found the packages, they were still wrapped up nice and neat. He had our narcotics agents pull in the usual suspects of dealers and users. Several of the local users said they received word from Larry that he was getting a shipment in on the Fourth. The consensus was that Larry would call when he got the stuff in, but they never heard from him. Most of them got their fixes from someone else that night and then the next day they heard about Larry getting shot."

I pondered what I'd just heard, flipping through the report as I did so. "Who was his supplier?"

Yates shrugged. "We were never real sure. We worked that angle for years, but haven't been able to identify his supplier."

"Did you find any money in the house?"

"Not a dime, which was why we believed Melissa left on her own. The way we figured it, she killed Larry, took all the money he'd made on his drug dealings, and then ran off to start a new life somewhere else."

"But why not take the drugs?" I asked.

"According to my snitch, Melissa didn't know anything about his dealings."

"How could she live with a man and not know what he was up to?"

Yates shook his head. "My snitch said Larry always sent Melissa to the back bedroom when anyone dropped by to make a deal. She said Larry was always very secretive. He would talk in whispers and kept his stash concealed in that gym bag. It was always by his side."

"But he was dead, so why didn't Melissa take the bag? For all she knew, it was loaded with money."

"She probably didn't want to touch her dead husband. After he was shot, Larry had slumped over and come to rest on top of the bag, so she would've had to pull his body off the bag to get to it. Besides, I imagine she was in a hurry to get out of there after what she'd just done."

I dug around in the file box until I found a thick packet of crime scene photos. They were printed on traditional four-by-six photo paper. I began sifting through them, and the crime scene came alive for me. The entire house was tidy, so the search must've been easy to conduct.

Larry's body was slumped onto his right side on the couch. There were five red blotches on the front of his shirt that highlighted the location of his bullet wounds. I held the photo close to my face but could barely see the gym bag under his torso. He was a heavy fellow, as one would expect from a corn-fed country boy, so it made sense that Melissa might not have been able to get the bag out from under him.

One of the subsequent photographs showed the bullet hole in the wall behind the sofa. It was about a foot above the top of the sofa and directly in line with where Larry's body would've been when he was seated upright.

"The bullet in the wall must've just missed his head."

Yates nodded. "The sheriff thought that was the first shot and it was meant for his face. We believe he lunged upward and took the next five shots in his chest, which caused him to fall back to a seated position, where he then slumped over on his side."

According to the medical examiner's report, Larry had taken one bullet to the heart, two to the left lung, one to the far left side of his chest, and one in the abdomen.

"No shell casings?" I asked.

"Not a one. It led us to believe the killer used a revolver."

I didn't see any holes in the sofa that would've lined up with the trajectories of the bullets. "Did any of the bullets pass through and through his body?"

"No, they were all removed from the body during autopsy."

I found the evidence recovery sheet and examined it, locating the five bullets that were recovered from the autopsy. They were listed as "undetermined caliber". I ran my finger down the entire list and frowned, turning it over to see if there was a backside.

"What's the matter?" Yates asked when he saw the expression on my face. "It's all there."

"Where's the bullet that went through the wall? It's not on the evidence sheet."

He sighed, rubbing his face. "That bullet was a pain in our asses. The sheriff made us tear that place apart three times looking for it, but we never did find it. If you look through the photographs, you'll see that we tore up every piece of furniture and scanned every inch of the floor and walls in the master bedroom, but we didn't find it."

I flipped through the photos until I found a picture of the master bedroom. The bed frame on the queen-sized bed would have been in line with the trajectory, unless the bullet glanced off of something inside the wall. To the left of the queen bed was a baby crib. "Did y'all search the baby bed?"

"We searched every inch of that room. We even cut open the mattresses and separated the stuffing from the springs and ran a metal detector across the stuffing to make sure we didn't miss anything." He paused and nodded his head. "I tell you, if that bullet would've been in that room, we would've found it."

"Did y'all consider the possibility it was carried away?"

"We did. In fact, the sheriff thought it got stuck in the sole of one of our boots and it was carried off that way. He made us retrace our steps in search of it, but we never did find it."

That was certainly a possibility. "What if there was a second victim and it was carried off that way?"

Yates rubbed his face in thought. "What do you mean?"

"Well, I was looking through the report and saw that there was a history of abuse. It seems Larry would beat Melissa on a regular basis."

"Just about every time he'd get drunk, but when our patrol deputies would go out there Melissa would deny it. She'd claim she'd fallen or hurt herself moving furniture or some other hogwash story. I think Fowler moved them close to his house because he thought Larry wouldn't dare touch Melissa if he was just down the road."

"If she finally had enough of the beatings and shot him in self-defense, who could blame her?"

"That's what the sheriff has been screaming for years, but Fowler doesn't want to even consider the fact that his daughter might've shot Larry. He won't even acknowledge the beatings, because that would give his daughter motive and make her a prime suspect."

"But if all of that were true, why would she run?"

"Because she just committed a murder."

"Not if it was self-defense." I spread the photographs out on the table so I could better recreate the scene in my mind. "When women kill their husbands because of abuse, they don't usually haul ass. They typically call nine-one-one and either claim it was an accident or they offer a compelling reason for the killing, but they don't usually disappear."

"So, you don't think she did it?"

"I'm not ready to exonerate her just yet, but I do think there was a second victim."

"A second victim?" Yates scoffed. "Who?"

"The baby."

Yates stared at me for a long moment as though he'd just seen the antichrist. "By all accounts, that woman loved her baby. She'd never kill her child. In all my years, I've never worked a case where a woman took the life of her own child. Mountain women are not made that way."

"I'm not saying it was on purpose." I slid the photo that depicted the exit bullet hole into the bedroom and stabbed at it with my finger. "This is the right height to hit a baby in that crib. The angle's a little off, but I didn't see where y'all put a rod through the hole to determine the exact angle. Did y'all?"

He shook his head and remained silent.

"If the bullet glanced off of a stud or a nail it could've changed course and hit the baby, which would explain why you couldn't find it. The bullet would've been removed from the scene when Melissa took the baby out of there."

Yates shook his head. "We checked every hospital in the state of Tennessee and North Carolina and in the northern portions of Alabama and Georgia, but no woman or child were admitted with injuries."

"If she murdered her husband and accidentally shot her baby, she wouldn't go to a hospital because they would immediately call the police and she would be arrested."

Yates stared down at the photographs. "But where's all the blood? If the baby would've been shot, wouldn't there have been blood in the crib?"

I plucked the close-up photograph of the crib from the pack and handed it to him. "What's wrong with this picture?"

He stared blankly at it and then shrugged. "There's no blood?"

"No, there aren't any blankets or sheets on the mattress. It's bare." I lifted the photo of Larry's shirt. "Notice how the blood was confined to the front of his shirt?" When Yates nodded, I continued. "That's because the entry wound was small enough that it didn't allow much blood to be spilled. If the baby was hit with a small caliber round that had already passed through and through a wall, the bullet would most likely enter the body and stay there. If Melissa ripped the blankets and sheets from the bed and wrapped them around the baby, it would've contained the blood."

Yates' eyes narrowed as they moved from one photograph to the other. After studying them for a bit, he nodded slowly. "So, you think it's possible Melissa carried the sixth bullet out with the baby?"

"If she was the shooter, I do think it's possible she hit the baby, and that would explain why she fled the scene. If someone else did the shooting, it's possible they took her hostage and carried the baby away with her." I flipped through the stack of photographs in my hand. "Where are the pictures of the projectiles removed from Larry's body?"

Yates reached into the box. After shuffling some files and envelopes around, he handed me another packet of pictures. "These are from the autopsy."

I removed the pictures from the envelope and went through them. When I came to the photo of the bullets that had been removed from Larry's body, I cursed out loud.

"What is it?" Yates asked.

I held up the photo of the five elongated projectiles that had been recovered from Larry Cooper's body. "The gun that killed Larry Cooper eighteen years ago in your county...it's the same gun that killed Fowler Underwood two weeks ago in my town."

CHAPTER 39

My mind raced on the drive to the county jail to see Junior. The uniquely identifying shape of the bullets from Larry's murder was identical to that of the bullets from Fowler's murder. While it was definitely the same weapon, how could I prove it was the same shooter? As I tried to figure out a way to link the shooters so long after the fact, an idea suddenly occurred to me. The more I mulled it over, the more I liked it.

What if Fowler had killed Larry with that revolver eighteen years earlier? He had motive—or, rather, justification. Hell, I'd expect any father of a daughter who was being beaten to take action. (Maybe not go as far as murdering the scumbag, but I'd certainly expect them to intercede on behalf of their daughters.) What if Fowler drove to Mechant Loup to find his daughter and ended up pulling that same revolver on someone? What if that someone had disarmed him and killed him with his own weapon? That would certainly explain the connection between the two cases, but who'd he pull the gun on? Did he believe he had found the person who'd kidnapped his daughter and grandchild?

I slowed and swerved to avoid a large rock that had fallen in the roadway, then sped up and zipped around the curve ahead. I needed to find out what Junior knew and I needed to get back home. I glanced at the flyer beside me in the center console—the one I had gotten from Sheriff Burns. There were four pictures on the front of the page; a small baby boy on the top left, an age progression picture on the top right of the same baby boy, a young woman on the bottom left, and an age progression picture of the same woman on the bottom right.

I could see a slight resemblance to Burton and Judith Vincent in the age progression portraits of Melissa Cooper and Baby Drake, but it was also possible it wasn't them.

I was still trying to figure out how things had gone sideways with Fowler and how the two cases were connected when I arrived at the Blackshaw County Detention Center. Yates had called in a favor for me and I was seated across from Junior within minutes.

"Who the hell are you?" Junior scratched at his leathery face. "The guard said you were from Louisiana. I don't know anybody from Louisiana."

The lines in Junior's skin were deep enough to hide a platoon of Chihuahuas. His hair was long and thin and patches of his beard looked like it had been dipped in white paint. I glanced down at my notes. He was a year younger than me. *Damn, I hope I don't look that old.*

I looked back up at Junior. After introducing myself, I delivered the bad news about his dad. His expression didn't change.

"On behalf of the Town of Mechant Loup," I said, "I'm sorry for your loss and I regret we couldn't identify him earlier."

His face twisted into a nasty scowl. "My pop died the day my sister disappeared."

I blinked. "Excuse me?"

"Melissa was always his favorite child. She could do no wrong." He shook his head in disdain. "Even when she hooked up with that drug-dealing fool, Larry, my dad refused to believe his little Princess was anything but perfect. And when she went missing, he acted as though he lost his only child. Mom, too. I was invisible to them when Melissa disappeared."

Junior paused long enough to cough violently into his hands. His eyes smarted. He wiped his mouth on his orange jumpsuit and then continued. "Do you know how it feels to wake up at fifteen and all of a sudden have to do everything for yourself? Mom and Pop were always depressed and didn't seem to want to do anything with me. I quit school and they didn't even know about it. I went hungry half the time, and when I did eat it was something I'd killed, cleaned, and cooked myself. The only time they spoke to me was to bitch at me for doing something wrong, and that was only if they were around." He grunted. "If you came here thinking I'd feel bad about the old man dying, you've got something else coming."

"No, I was hoping you'd know why he was in Louisiana and could maybe tell me who might want him dead."

I thought Junior was going to tell me to get lost, but he finally sighed and leaned his elbows on the table that separated us. "All I know is he came visit me about a month ago to tell me he got a big break in the case. He said he received a phone call from a Louisiana area code in early August and the person who called said they had seen Drake and that he was all grown up now."

"Drake...he's your sister's baby, right?"

Junior nodded. "He was almost a year old when they disappeared. Anyway, Pops said he kept calling the number back trying to get someone to answer, but no one would. He tried looking the number up on the Internet, but he couldn't find anything. He asked one of his buddies at the sheriff's department to look up the number, but they wouldn't do it without a warrant.

"He kept trying to call the number and, finally, somebody answered. It was some lady who said she was walking by a payphone and heard it ringing. He asked her where it was and she gave him the name of the grocery store. It was a weird name..." He let his voice trail off and stared up at the ceiling. Finally, he shook his head. "I can't think of it."

"Mechant Groceries?"

"That sounds right." Junior nodded. "I believe that's it. Well, he said he stopped by to let me know he was heading to Louisiana to find Melissa. I really think he thought I'd be happy."

I thought I saw Junior's eyes glistening, but he lowered his head and his long hair concealed most of his face.

"Did your dad have a gun?" I asked.

"Sure. He had lots of guns."

"What about a revolver? Maybe a .38 caliber?"

"He's got three or four revolvers. One of them might be a .38. Why?"

"Well, it appears he was killed with a .38 revolver and I was wondering if he might've been killed with his own gun."

"I couldn't tell you."

I continued questioning Junior, but he didn't know more than I'd already learned about the incident. I pulled the flyer I'd received from Sheriff Burns and slid it across the table. "How old was your sister in this picture?"

"She was eighteen." He frowned again. "Pops didn't want to give up hope—and he never did—but I was sure she had been murdered. Of course, it was hard to imagine anyone killing Drake and I thought he might still be out there somewhere." His face softened when he mentioned Drake. "He was such a cool little kid. He was just starting to try to crawl when they disappeared. I missed him a lot at first. I used to have fun playing with him and I looked forward to being an uncle. It made me feel important. I often wonder if Drake knows he has an uncle. If he even remembers me, you know?"

I was tempted to ask about his own kids and why he wasn't doing a better job caring for them, but I resisted the urge. Instead, I asked if Larry Cooper had any relatives who might know something about the case. He told me Larry had a brother named Moe who lived on the outskirts of Gatlinburg, near where the Roaring Forks Motor Trail began. "He operates a fly fishing bait shop around those parts."

I didn't remember the address I'd found for Moe, but it wasn't in Gatlinburg. After he gave me the directions to Moe's house, I thanked him for his time and told him I'd do everything I could to find the person who killed his dad. He nodded his head and I thought I saw tears pool in his eyes, but he turned away before I could be sure.

When I left the detention center, I drove straight to Moe's house and found him in an old building tying thread to a hook. He looked up from the giant magnifying glass that was mounted to the table. I didn't waste any time introducing myself or explaining the reason I was there.

He slowly lowered the fly-tying equipment with which he was working, removed a pair of glasses from his head, and mopped his forehead with a thin hand. "I haven't heard Larry's name spoken in years and now, all of a sudden, I'm hearing it two times in two weeks."

"Did Fowler Underwood get in touch with you?"

"Yeah, the old man told me he was close to finding Melissa. He told me once he located Melissa he would find out who killed my brother." Moe sighed heavily. "I told him I already knew who killed my brother—that hateful little daughter of his. I'm not going to pretend Larry was an angel. Sure, he used to knock her around a bit, but that didn't give her the right to shoot him full of holes while he sat on the sofa. I don't believe in a man hitting a woman, but that's what the law is for. She could've called the sheriff or even come to me and I would've put a stop to it...but to shoot a defenseless man?" He shook his head. "She didn't have to go doing that. I had half a mind to follow Fowler and turn Melissa in myself when he found her."

I studied Moe for a long minute before asking, "Did you follow him?"

"No. I'm too busy to go chasing ghosts."

"When was it that Fowler came by to visit?"

"Two Fridays ago."

I furrowed my brow. "Are you sure it was two Fridays ago—September twenty-third? That's the day we believe Fowler was killed."

Moe shrugged. "It could've been three weeks ago. I didn't really make a note of it."

I nodded. If I didn't write down times and dates, I couldn't remember much of anything. We talked for a while longer about his relationship with his brother and then I asked if I could collect his DNA. He cocked his head to the side and fixed me with a hard stare.

"What the hell for?" he asked.

When I explained, he pursed his lips and nodded. "If it'll help clear this up," he said, "I'm happy to do it."

CHAPTER 40

8:00 a.m., Wednesday, October 5

Susan rolled on top of me and pressed her thick, bare breasts against my chest. "I couldn't sleep Monday night without you."

I had a hard time dragging my eyelids open, but I nodded my agreement. After driving all afternoon and evening, I had finally rolled into Mechant Loup a little after midnight last night and found Susan waiting up for me at home. We had made love until late into the morning and then fell asleep in each other's arms. I think she drooled on my face in her sleep, because I heard her mumble an apology as she wiped the side of my face with the sheet.

I chuckled to myself and rubbed my hands along her smooth body. "I need to get up but I don't want to," I said. "I could sleep for a week."

"Well, I have to get a run in before I head to the office, so…" She kissed me and pushed off of the bed. "If you're not up when I get back, I'm going to pour a pitcher of ice water on your face."

I rolled to my stomach and pulled a pillow over my head. *Just five more minutes,* I thought. *And then I'll be ready to get up.*

I jerked when the door slammed, but then settled back into the soft mattress. I was just dozing off when the house phone rang. I groaned and rolled to the edge of the bed so I could reach it. I pulled it to my ear and said hello. It was Susan's mom.

"Mrs. Wilson, how are you?" I sat up in the bed and glanced out the window. Susan was already disappearing down Paradise Place. "Susan just left for her morning run."

"I'm actually calling to speak with you," she said in her soft and frail voice.

"Me?" I cocked my head sideways. "Okay, what's up?"

She was quiet for a long moment and I was about to ask if she was still there, but she finally spoke again. "I need your help."

"Sure…anything."

"I need to know how to acquire a ticket for Susan's fight."

My heart leapt in my chest. "Are you serious?"

"I'm scared to death, but I'm very serious." She cleared her throat. "It'll be my baby's last fight, so I think I need to be there to support her. As you know, I can't stand the thought of her being hit, so it'll be quite troubling for me, but I want her to know I'm there for her."

I was beaming. "I'll get you a ticket. We're getting a room in Houston, so you can stay with us."

"That would be lovely."

After chatting for a few more minutes, we ended the conversation and I took a shower. By the time I got out, Susan was back from her run and she was blending a breakfast shake. Achilles sat on the kitchen floor eagerly watching her. I didn't know why, because she never gave him a sip.

I shoved my paddle holster into my khaki pants and walked up behind her. She hadn't heard me approaching because of the noisy blender and she jerked a little when I ran my fingers across her neck. She shut off the blender and leaned her head back to kiss me.

"Heading into the office already?" she asked.

"Do you have an extra ticket for your fight?" I already knew the answer, because she always reserved one for her mom. And without fail, her mom never showed up. While she had grown somewhat accustomed to being disappointed and she usually played it off, I knew that deep down it hurt her feelings.

"I have three." She removed the pitcher and drank straight from it. When she pulled the pitcher away from her face, the contents left a green mustache across her lips. "Why? Who wants to come?"

"Guess." I tried to keep a straight face, but it was no use.

She slammed the pitcher to the counter and Achilles recoiled in surprise. "No way!"

"Yes way." I smiled. "Your mom's coming."

Susan leapt straight into the air and into my arms, nearly sending me sprawling. She squeezed my neck so hard I thought I was going to have to tap out. When she released her death grip on me, she asked how I knew. I told her about the phone call and then I told her I had to leave.

"What's your next move?" she asked.

I paused near the door, thinking the obvious. "Fowler Underwood followed that phone call to Mechant Loup and that led him to Burton Vincent. Whatever he found down Dire Lane got him killed, so I'm heading back to that neighborhood to see if I can find it too."

"Just as long as you don't get yourself killed."

CHAPTER 41

I spent all morning walking the woods behind Dire Lane. I wanted to make sure I hadn't missed anything and I knew it would be fruitless to start knocking on doors in the morning, so my plan was to wait until after three when kids started returning from school. At about noon I drove out of the neighborhood to eat, and then returned at two. It still looked like a ghost town. Knowing the buses would be by soon and wanting very much to speak with Burton Vincent again, and alone, I parked at the back of the street to wait.

Thirty minutes later I saw the first bus turn down the street a mile away. I pulled out my binoculars and dialed up the focus, watching as the bus stopped intermittently on its way to the back. When it arrived in front of the Vincent residence, it stopped and the side door unfolded. Burton, a blue mesh backpack strung over his left arm, lumbered down the steps and dropped to the street. He turned and hollered something at a kid who was hanging out of a window, and then turned toward his house.

Dropping my binoculars, I shoved the gearshift in *drive* and raced toward his house. After I passed the bus, I glanced in my side mirror and saw Paul Rupe step off at the last house in the back. He stared after my Tahoe and I saw him stop walking when I turned into Burton's driveway.

"Hey, Burton," I called as I dropped from my Tahoe. "I need to talk with you."

Burton, who had already ascended the steps and was unlocking the front door, stopped and turned at the sound of my voice. He let his backpack fall to the porch and walked back toward the edge of the steps. "Is it about Troy? I've already told you everything I know about him."

I tucked my file folder under my arm and ambled toward him. "No," I said when I was standing in front of him on the porch. "It's about the phone call and that missing person flyer."

He nodded, a look of concern spreading over his face. "Are we going to be in trouble for making that prank call?"

"No." I pulled out the flyer I'd received from Sheriff Burns. "Is this the same kind of flyer Paul gave you?"

"Yes, sir." Burton didn't even hesitate. "That's the one. He says my mom and I look like them people, but I don't think so."

"What about anyone you know?" I asked. "Do they look familiar to you at all?"

He studied the pictures slowly, then shook his head. "No, sir. I don't recognize them at all."

I shoved the picture back in the folder and tucked it under my arm. After pulling a sealed buccal swab packet from my rear pocket, I held it up. "Do you know what this is?"

Burton shook his head from side to side.

I explained what it was and told him why I wanted to collect his DNA. His eyes widened.

"You don't really think that's me on the poster, do you?" he asked. "Paulie brought that here as a joke. He didn't really believe it was me."

"Well, I'd like to know for sure and there's only one way to find out."

He shuffled his feet and shoved both hands in the front pockets of his uniform pants. "I...I mean, I don't know if I should do it."

If Judith Vincent really was Melissa Cooper, she'd never allow him to freely surrender his DNA, and I didn't think a judge would sign a search warrant forcing the issue, so I needed his permission to collect the sample.

"Look, you read the poster. This woman and her son are missing and endangered. Someone apparently thinks you're this Drake fellow and your mom's Melissa, and that fact alone has resulted in the murders of two people—one of whom just so happens to have been your sister's boyfriend." I paused to let him think about it. "A quick DNA test can clear this all up. We both know it's not you, so we need to do the test and convince the killer you're not Drake Cooper, which will also prove your mom is not Melissa Cooper."

Burton's eyes widened a little. "You think the killer's coming after me and Mom next?"

"It's hard to say, but I think it's important to remove both of you from the situation."

He glanced down at the packet in my hand. "Will it hurt?"

"I'll literally be rubbing a long cotton swab against the inside of your cheeks. It'll hurt as much as it hurts to run your tongue along the inside of your mouth."

He hesitated a bit longer, then nodded his head. "Okay, I'll do it."

Once I'd swabbed both cheeks and secured the cotton swabs in the evidence tubes, I asked Burton not to discuss our conversation with anyone.

"Not even my parents? Not even my mom?"

"Normally, I would never advise kids to keep things from their parents, but in this case, I'd like you to keep this conversation between the two of us." I raised an eyebrow. "Don't even tell Kegan or Paul, who happens to be standing in his driveway right now watching us talk."

Burton's head jerked toward the back of the street and he huffed when he saw Paul still standing in his driveway watching us. "He probably thinks we're all going to jail for the phone call."

"You can tell him I assured you that won't happen. As far as I'm concerned, the prank call is a closed case."

He nodded and then stared down at his shoes. His brow was furrowed and he seemed troubled.

"What is it?" I asked.

Keeping his head tilted downward, he lifted his eyes to stare at me through his eyebrows. "What if your test says I am Drake Cooper? What then?"

That was a good question and I didn't want to answer it, so I just told him not to worry about it. "Like you said, you don't even look like the kid."

CHAPTER 42

After leaving Dire Lane, I stopped by the office to pick up some evidence submittal forms and then drove straight to the La Mort Police Department Crime Lab. I dropped off the DNA swabs from Fowler Underwood, Jr. and Burton Vincent, and asked for an expedited analysis.

"This is for an open homicide investigation and I need to know if these two men are related," I said. "I don't want to be pushy, but I need this done yesterday."

The analyst told me she'd do her best, but said it would be Friday at the earliest, but more than likely not until Monday. Apparently, there were a few cases ahead of me that were equally important. I thanked her and—after stopping at a store in the city—drove home. It was nearly nine o'clock when I finally pulled into my driveway.

I checked in on Susan, who was sparring with Takecia under Damian's watchful eyes, and then took Achilles for a ride to the shelter. During a break in her sparring, Susan had asked me to check on Allie and Sammy. Achilles ran around the perimeter of the building checking for dangers while I ambled up the steps and walked inside. Sammy was sitting on his mom's lap and they were watching television in the living room when I entered.

Allie started to stand up, but I waved for her not to bother. "Susan wanted me to come back here and check on y'all—see if you needed anything."

She smiled and shook her head. "Everything's perfect. It's the first time I've felt safe in years."

"I love my new fake house!" Sammy wore a Winnie the Pooh pajama shirt with a matching bottom. "It's the best time ever!"

I laughed and waved for him to step forward. He did and I pulled my hand from behind my back and held up a plastic bag.

"Do you know what's in here?" I asked.

His eyes lit up as he nodded his head. "A Christmas present!"

"It's not Christmas, honey," Allie called from the sofa. "It's just a present."

I opened the bag and removed the model cop car from inside. "This is a smaller version of the police Chevy Tahoe that Chief Wilson drives," I explained. "It's late tonight, but when I get off work tomorrow afternoon you and I can start building this thing together."

"Can Mommy help?" he asked, his eyes growing wide with excitement. "I bet she knows how to build a shelfy taco."

Allie laughed and explained to Sammy that she would be doing some training with Susan while we work on the model car. "Chief Wilson is going to teach Mommy how to defend herself," she explained. "And then I'll be able to keep both of us safe."

That seemed to settle it for Sammy and he followed me to the door as I left. When I stepped out onto the porch, he pointed and asked if he could ride Achilles. The last time I laughed so hard and felt so much joy was when Abigail was around.

"Well, his back's not strong enough for a big man like you to ride," I said. "But maybe one day we can find you a real horse to ride."

"Yay!" He jumped up and down and pretended to be riding an imaginary horse. "I'm a cowboy."

Allie had gotten up from the sofa and was standing behind Sammy and watching him bounce around in the doorway. When she looked up at me, her eyes were misty. "Thank you so much for everything." She pushed her lips together to stop from crying. "Please tell Chief Wilson how much I appreciate what y'all are doing for us."

"It's been a lifelong dream of hers," I said. "It's her pleasure."

Achilles bounded along beside me and licked my hand on the walk back to my Tahoe.

CHAPTER 43

Two days later…

It was three o'clock on Friday afternoon when I got the call. I'd been poring over the murder files and going over the surveillance footage from Mr. Pellegrin all day and, just minutes before three, I thought I had a minor breakthrough.

"Susan!" I'd called from my office. "Can you come in here?"

She had walked in and pulled a chair as close to mine as possible without sitting in my lap. "What is it?"

"When we watched these videos the first time, we were looking for anything that was there and didn't belong."

Susan nodded. "That's how we found the blue Nissan."

"Right." I spread out my notes detailing the traffic from each of the days depicted on the surveillance videos. "We should've been looking for what *wasn't* there."

"What do you mean?" She leaned closer, studying the detailed lists of traffic from the neighborhood.

I pointed to Thursday, September 22. "On this day, forty-one cars from the neighborhood left the street in the morning and they all returned in the afternoon—not counting delivery trucks and school buses. And the same thing is true for every other day of the week, except for Friday, the day Fowler's vehicle disappeared back there."

Susan compared the lists and stabbed at the page with her index finger. "This black Jeep Grand Cherokee didn't leave the neighborhood on Friday."

"That's right." I leaned back and folded my arms across my chest. "And do you know who drives a black Jeep Grand Cherokee?"

She was thoughtful. After about ten seconds, she nodded slowly. "Judith Vincent."

"When Fowler Underwood drove back there that morning, Judith was the only one in the entire neighborhood who was home. She's the only one who could've killed Fowler."

I'd already told Susan what I'd learned in Tennessee about Melissa Cooper and, although she'd agreed the portrait didn't look exactly like Judith, she surmised the artist could've gotten it slightly wrong. "I've seen a number of these age progression photos over the years and some nail it while others totally miss the mark," she had commented.

I snatched up a driver's license photo of Judith that I'd printed from the DMV database and placed it on my desk beside the flyer of Melissa Cooper. "It could be her."

Susan rested her arm on my shoulder as she leaned in to study it, and that was when the phone rang. It was the crime lab and they had the results of the DNA comparison.

"What'd you find?" I asked the analyst, holding my breath.

She began talking about how she had extracted a profile from each sample and performed an avuncular DNA analysis. She explained that this test was used to determine if an individual is the biological aunt or uncle of a child. She then began citing numbers of probability and other technical information. I didn't want to be rude, but I cut her off.

"In layman's terms, please—are they related?"

She grunted. "Without a doubt, Moe Cooper is in Burton Vincent's paternal lineage. He's the kid's uncle, which would make his brother the father."

After asking her to fax a copy of the lab report, I sank into my chair and replaced the handset.

"What's up?" Susan asked. "Is Burton the missing kid?"

I nodded slowly. "That means his mom is Melissa Cooper and she's a murder suspect."

Susan and I were both silent for a few minutes as we processed the new information. I was trying to figure out my next move and wondered if I should involve the Blackshaw County Sheriff's Department. Burns had sworn out a warrant for Melissa's arrest and warrants were good until served, but that warrant might've been recalled after Burns removed himself from office.

"Poor kid," Susan finally said, breaking the silence between us. "He gets to find out his name isn't really Burton, Rick isn't really his dad, his mom is a murder suspect, and she's accused of killing his biological father." She shook her head. "His world is about to be destroyed."

"Baylor said Burton jokes that Cindy is his adopted sister." I frowned. "This is a cruel dose of karma."

"Do you think Rick knows?"

"He has to know he's not Burton's dad, but I doubt Melissa admitted to killing her ex-husband."

"If she did, he's a brave man for marrying her anyway."

"Brave—or stupid." I glanced at the clock. Rick and Judith would still be at work, so I should be able to catch Burton home alone. I asked Susan if she could pick up Judith from her work while I met with Burton. "She works at the water plant on Cypress Highway."

"What if she refuses to come with me?" Susan asked. "She could tell me to go screw myself."

"Tell her I've brought Burton to the station and I need to speak with her about him. Maybe she'll agree to follow you here. That shouldn't throw up any red flags."

Susan was thoughtful. "If she really is Melissa Cooper and she's the one who killed Fowler, then that means she killed her own dad. If she's willing to do that, she'll stop at nothing to keep her secret."

Susan had a point. Although I didn't need to say it, I told her to be careful when we parted ways in the parking lot. As she headed toward the east side of town, I headed north to Dire Lane. I tried to rehearse what I would tell Burton, but I was still unsure of what to say when I pulled into the driveway of his house. Cindy was sitting on the front porch swing when I arrived. She looked sad.

She watched as I stepped out of my Tahoe and walked up the steps. I stopped on the landing and smiled. "Are you okay?"

Her chin trembled. She opened her mouth to talk, but clamped it shut as her emotions got the best of her. I wanted to tell her it would get easier with time, but that's not what she needed to hear right now.

"If you ever have any questions,"—I dug out one of the business cards that Mayor Cain had gotten printed up for me and handed it to her—"call anytime."

She nodded her thanks.

I shot a thumb toward the door. "Is Burton here?"

"Yes, sir." She stood from the swing and walked to the door. "I'll get him."

When Burton stepped outside and saw it was me, he stopped in his tracks. "The test?"

I frowned. "I'm sorry, son, but it's true…you're Drake Cooper."

He leaned back against the door frame to steady himself. His mouth dropped open and he stared absently at me. His mouth moved in a futile attempt to speak. I could tell he was trying hard to stay strong. Finally, he managed to ask what would happen. "I mean, what does it all mean? What happens now? Does my mom know? What about my dad?"

"I know you have a lot of questions. Let's go down to the station so we can talk."

He nodded weakly and closed the door behind him, followed me down the steps.

CHAPTER 44

Judith Vincent's car was already in front of the building when I pulled up to my parking spot under the police department. He saw the car and his face turned even paler than it was already.

"Does my mom know about the results of the test?" His voice quivered.

"No." I pulled out my phone and texted Susan, asking her to keep Judith away from my office. She texted back immediately and said Judith was in an interview room on the opposite side of the building. I waved for Burton to follow me. "Let's get up to my office so we can sort this thing out."

Once we were seated in my office and I had moved the model Tahoe that Sammy and I had built to the side, I asked Burton what he knew about his mom.

He looked at the missing person flyer on my desk and tapped it with his fingers. "I don't understand how this can really be me or my mom. My mom's from here, in Mechant Loup. My grandparents— her mom and dad—are from Upper Chateau. I was born at Chateau General. I've never even been to Tennessee and my mom and dad have never mentioned we were from there."

I scowled. "So, your mom's mom and dad are from Upper Chateau?"

He nodded.

"What about your dad...Rick? What do you know about his past?"

"He's also from here, and so are my grandparents on his side. We go to Central Chateau to see them all the time." He looked up at me, his eyes searching mine. "If I am Drake Cooper, is my dad... Does my dad have a different name, too?"

"Unless y'all are in a witness protection program, I'm afraid this test proves Rick Vincent is not your dad. You two aren't related at all."

Burton bit down hard and I thought he was going to cry, but he managed to hold it together. "Who's my real dad? I mean, what's his name? What's he do for a living? Where's he been all my life? Is he cool?"

"His name was Larry Cooper."

"*Was* Larry Cooper? Has he changed his name?"

"No. I'm afraid he's gone. He was murdered when you were little."

Tears forced their way through Burton's squeezed eyelids. His face twisted in anger as he tried to fight back the flood that was coming. "How did I not know any of this?" Saliva sprayed from his mouth as he struggled to get the question out. "Why didn't my mom or dad tell me any of this? I've gone my whole life believing a lie!"

My heart broke for Burton. The tough mischievous kid I'd first met had been reduced to a bag of bones and sorrow. In an instant, his world had been turned upside down. I walked around my desk to sit beside him. After putting a hand on his shoulder, I just sat in silence while he sobbed quietly, trying his best to fight it.

"What happened?" he managed to ask after a while. "How was he murdered?"

"He was shot in his home in Birchtown, Tennessee." I paused for a second, trying not to give him too much information at once. "The sheriff who investigated the case believes you were there at the time of the shooting."

"Me?" He wiped his eyes and looked up. "I was there when my dad was murdered?"

I nodded. "You would've been about ten months old."

Burton sniffled. "I was too young to remember anything."

"Do you have a scar anywhere on your body?" I asked. "Something that would've been there as long as you could remember?"

"No, sir. Why?"

"Well, there's some indication you might've been hit during the gunfire."

"You think I was shot? With a gun?"

"There's a possibility you were hit by one of the bullets meant for your dad. It would be a small scar, probably looks like a dimple by now."

He shook his head. "I don't have any scars like that. I mean, I have some scars, but I remember where they all came from."

I asked him to stand and lift up his shirt and I shined a light on his stomach and back, searching for pinpoint scars. There were none. After lowering his shirt, he held his arms out with his palms up, and then turned them over. Nothing. I waved for him to return to his chair.

I leaned back in my seat and rubbed my face, trying to make sense out of everything I knew. As I moved the pieces of the puzzle around in my mind, a picture started to slowly emerge. I cursed inwardly, hoping I was wrong. If I was right, this kid was an army without a country…a ship without a flag.

Wanting to keep Burton talking, I leaned forward, dug out my cell phone, and scrolled through my images. On Tuesday, when I had gone through the old case file at the sheriff's department, I'd taken snapshots of some of the pictures in it. I continued scrolling until I found the one I'd snapped of Larry Cooper. It was the last photograph taken of him before he died and it showed him sitting on the steps of his trailer holding his son—who we now knew was Burton—in his lap.

"This is you and your dad," I said, handing the phone to Burton. "This was taken a day or two before he was killed."

Burton pulled my phone close to his face and used his thumbs to enlarge the image. He blinked away the blurriness in his eyes. "I look like him."

"You do."

When Burton handed me the phone, his brow furrowed. "If everything you're telling me is true, then my dad—Rick—knows I'm not his son."

"That's correct."

"I've been joking with Cindy for years, telling her she was adopted." His face twisted into a sour smile as the irony of the situation hit him. "As it turns out, I'm the one who's adopted."

He was right. For him to be carrying Rick Vincent's last name, he had to have been adopted, but how much did Rick know about his wife? At what point in Burton's life had Rick and Judith met? I had a lot of questions for Judith Vincent, and I needed to meet with her as soon as possible to iron them out.

"Do you mind hanging out with Chief Wilson?" I asked Burton. "I need to speak with your mom."

"Yes, sir," he said, but then hesitated. "Um, you said my real father was killed—murdered."

I nodded.

"But you didn't tell me who did it."

CHAPTER 45

Judith Vincent looked up at me when I stepped into the interview room. Worry lines were etched across her face. "What's going on?" she asked. "Chief Wilson said you needed to speak with me about something, but I've been sitting here waiting and no one has told me a thing. Where's Burton? Why do you have him here?"

I placed my file folder on the desk and sat across from her. I had activated the audio and video recorder before entering the room, so I didn't bother pulling out a digital recorder.

"So, what's going on?" she repeated when I didn't say anything.

I decided not to waste any time. Pulling the flyer from my case file, I slid it to her. "Do you recognize these people?"

Her face tightened, but she tried to act casual. "One of Burton's friends gave this to him. He thought it looked like us, but I don't believe it does."

I extended the flyer out where I could perform a side-by-side comparison. "I don't know, ma'am. This woman looks very similar to you."

She took the flyer from my hand and stared at it. She scoffed and then handed it back. "She's got brown hair, brown eyes, and a pale complexion—that probably describes one third of the women in Louisiana. She looks nothing like me."

"So, are you saying that your son, Burton, is not this missing kid?"

She forced a chuckle. "Of course not."

"Very well, then, let me gather some information from you and hopefully we can clear up this whole mess."

"What mess?"

"Someone seems to think Burton is Drake Cooper all grown up." I made a show of flipping through my notes. I stopped on the first clean page I got to and looked up, my pen poised over the page. "Where was Burton born?"

"Excuse me?"

"Where'd you give birth to your son?"

"Why are you asking these questions?"

"Like I said before…I'm simply gathering some information so I can clear up this whole misunderstanding."

Judith took a subtle bite of her lower lip, then quickly said, "He was born at Chateau General."

I jotted down the information. "How long have you and Rick been married?"

"What does my marriage have to do with this missing kid?"

I cocked my head sideways. "Can you please indulge me so I can clear this matter up sooner rather than later?"

"If it'll get us out of here faster…" Judith huffed. "We've been married for eighteen years. Almost nineteen."

"How could you have been married to Rick Vincent for eighteen years when you were married to Larry Cooper eighteen years ago?" I wanted to ask, but didn't. "Where'd you meet Rick?"

"At my second cousin's wedding. He was best man to the groom and I was one of the bridesmaids. We were both drunk by the end of the night and I went home with him." She folded her arms across her breasts and stared pointedly at me. "Do you want the details?"

I ignored the sarcasm and continued. "When was Burton born?"

"The thirteenth of March. He turned seventeen a few months ago."

I studied Judith. *She must be lying about Burton's age, because he was six months old eighteen years ago.* "Have you ever cheated on Rick?"

She gasped. "What kind of question is that?"

"I mean, you don't have to answer it if you don't want to," I said slowly, "but it's a standard question in these types of investigations."

After glaring at me for a few long moments, she finally said she had never cheated on Rick.

I pushed my notepad aside and pulled out my phone. I scrolled through the images until I found the picture of Larry Cooper and his baby, turned it so she could see. "Do you recognize this guy?"

She shook her head.

"Would it surprise you to learn that this is Burton's real father?"

She scoffed. "That's utter nonsense. This is some kind of

investigative ploy to trick me into saying what you want to hear."

"No ploy at all, Judith." I lifted the phone again. "Are you sure you don't recognize this man? His name's Larry Cooper."

"Never seen him and never heard of him."

"Do you have a birth certificate for Burton?"

Judith's chin jutted out confidently. "I most certainly do."

"Whose name is listed as the father?"

I was surprised when she told me it was Rick Vincent, and she said it with confidence.

"There are those who might argue that Rick is not Burton's father."

She uncrossed her arms and placed her hands on the table, leaning forward for emphasis. "I'm Burton's mother, so they can argue all they want, but I'm the only one who can say who his father is."

I smiled just enough to get under her skin. "Well, as it turns out, I obtained a sample of Burton's DNA and had it compared to the DNA of Moe Cooper, who happens to be Larry Cooper's brother. You might remember Larry as the man you once married in Tennessee." I watched the color drain from Judith's face. Even her lips turned white. "I can tell by your expression that you already know the results." I planted my elbows on the desk and leaned forward myself. "Does Rick know your real name is Melissa and Burton's name is Drake?"

Judith had to work her mouth a few times before words spilled out. "I don't know who Drake is and I'm not Melissa. My name is Judith."

My eyes narrowed. I was pretty certain of these things: Judith had raised Drake Cooper to believe he was Burton Vincent; Drake's real father had been murdered; and Drake's real mother was either still missing or sitting right in front of me. If Judith didn't know Burton's real name, it might mean she was not Melissa. If she was not the missing woman, then where was Melissa? And what if Judith was playing me?

I asked Judith to give me a moment and I stepped into the hallway to send a text message to Susan, asking if she could have one of her officers find Rick Vincent and bring him to the station. She responded immediately to say she was sending someone right away.

I waited in the hallway until Susan texted me to say Amy was on her way to the Vincent home to get Rick, and then I rejoined Judith.

CHAPTER 46

"Good news," I told Judith. "We've got someone heading out to your house to pick up Rick. As soon as he gets here, he's going to clear this whole thing up for us."

Just when I thought Judith couldn't get any paler, her skin became almost transparent. "A cop is on the way to my house to get Rick?"

I nodded. "I'm sure he'll be interested to know that we have indisputable DNA evidence to prove his son is actually Drake Cooper and his wife is actually Melissa Cooper—a murderess wanted from Tennessee for killing her first husband."

Judith stammered for a few seconds. "I'm not Melissa Cooper. Look, you've got to believe me. I had nothing to do with a murder and I don't know anything about Drake Cooper. There's no need to involve Rick in this—"

"Burton *is* Drake, so you know a lot more than you're saying." I waved my hand dismissively. "But that's okay—Rick will help clear this whole mess up for me and, before long, you'll be sitting in a jail cell charged with murdering Larry Cooper, Fowler Underwood, and Troy Gandy." I stood to leave, but she jumped to her feet.

"Wait…please. Just give me a second to explain."

"Explain what?"

She licked her lips. "Look, I don't know anything about any murders and neither does Rick, but I do know something about Burton."

I slowly regained my seat and asked what she knew.

Judith took a deep breath—as though what she was about to say pained her—and then let it out. "While I love Burton like my own son, I'm not his mother."

"Is that so?" My interest was fully aroused. "If you're not his mother, then who is?"

"I don't know. When I first met Rick he told me he was a single father. He told me his wife had up and disappeared, leaving their six-month-old baby behind. He was left to raise Burton on his own and he's done a great job."

I studied Judith's face. "So, when you said earlier that you gave birth to Burton…?"

"I lied."

"Why?"

"I was trying to protect Burton. I don't want him to know his mother abandoned him. That kind of news can be devastating to a child. Everything else I said was true. I don't know anything about a murder and neither does Rick. If it's okay with you, I'd like to go home now. I have to get dinner started." She glanced over her shoulder. "Did your officer get to my house yet?"

"Why are you so worried about our officer getting to your house and why are you in such a hurry to leave?" I shook my head and leaned back in my chair. "You're not going anywhere. I don't know if you missed it, but I'm investigating two murders and you're my prime suspect."

"Me?" Judith recoiled in her chair, throwing her hands to her chest. "Why am I a suspect?"

"First off, since you're not Burton's mother, you're not Fowler's daughter, and that removes an element of doubt concerning your willingness to kill Fowler. Second, you're the only one with the opportunity to kill Fowler."

"Opportunity? What on earth do you mean?"

"Everyone who lives down Dire Lane went to work on the morning of the murder, except for you."

"I…I don't even know what day he was murdered."

"It was Friday, September twenty-third." I grunted. "You might not remember the date, but you remember the details, so why don't you cut the bull and tell me why you killed the poor old man?"

Judith licked her lips. "Can you call the officer and ask them to wait before going to my house? Rick is probably busy and he shouldn't be disturbed."

"Don't worry about Rick. He'll be down here shortly and he'll find out soon enough what you've done."

Tears began streaming down Judith's face. "Please, just tell your officer to turn around."

"No." I leaned closer to her. "Now, tell me why you killed Fowler Underwood."

"I didn't kill him, but I know who did." Judith didn't even bother wiping her face. She just allowed the tears to flow freely and splash on the desk in front of her. "I'll tell you everything if you just tell your officer to turn around and not bother Rick."

I cocked my head to the side. "Why are you so worried about Rick? And why do you keep asking if Amy arrived at your house yet?"

"Because he's got Cindy!"

"He's her dad, so why wouldn't he have her?"

"He's going to kill her if I talk!" She spat the words. "When I told him I was coming to the station, he said he wasn't going down without a fight. He said he was taking Cindy and he would kill her if I told y'all what he did, so I promised him I wouldn't say a thing. If you go looking for him, he's going to think I talked."

"Look, I know it was you who killed Fowler, because your car was the only car that didn't leave for work that Friday. You drive a black Jeep Grand Cherokee, don't you?"

She nodded, rubbing leakage from her nose. "But I didn't kill anyone. It was all Rick, but you can't do anything until Cindy is away from him. Please, just let me go home and act like everything's normal. When Cindy's away from him, then you can go after him."

"It couldn't have been Rick. He left for work that morning and he didn't get home until the afternoon, so it had to be you."

She shook her head. "I was in Rick's Mustang that day. He stayed home."

"What?" I watched her eyes closely, trying to determine if she was lying. "You know, all it'll take is one call to your work to find out if you were really—"

"Call them," she dared. "I was at work all day that Friday. Rick gets one three-day weekend each month, and that was his weekend off. I can tell you detail by detail what he did and I can show you proof, but I'm not saying a word until Cindy's safe."

Unsure if I should believe her, I stood slowly to my feet. "Do you really think he'd hurt Cindy?"

"He'd do anything to keep from going to prison, and I mean *any*thing. He won't even set foot in the police station. Why do you think he made me come here with Cindy last Friday?"

"Give me a minute." I stepped out into the hallway and threw the lock on the outside of the door so Judith couldn't leave. I rushed through the dispatcher's station and through the opposite hallway.

When I pushed open the door to my office, Susan and Burton looked up at me. I waved for Susan to meet me in the hallway.

"What's up?" she asked when we were alone.

"Did Amy find Rick?"

"I'm not sure." She pulled out her radio and called for Amy. Other than a little static, the radio was silent. She called again, but there was still no answer from Amy.

CHAPTER 47

After radioing that she had arrived at the Vincent residence on Dire Lane, Officer Amy Cooke stepped out of her patrol car and stood for a second surveying the house. She had been asked to contact Rick Vincent and have him accompany her to the police department for questioning. As far as everyone knew, he wasn't a suspect in anything, but two people had been murdered within a few miles of this place, so she wasn't taking any chances.

Keeping her right hand close to her weapon and her eyes trained on the front windows of the residence, Amy approached the steps that led to the elevated porch. The sun was dipping to the west and had already slid behind the distant trees, so it wasn't in her eyes.

She moved lightly up the steps and crossed the wooden porch to stand to the left side of the front door. There was a swing on the porch, but it was empty. Using her left hand, she knocked sharply on the door frame and waited. The house was above the ground—at least five feet, thanks to flood elevation requirements in the area—so she figured she'd hear footsteps if anyone moved around inside. After a few minutes of silence, she knocked again.

When there was no movement from inside, Amy made her way down the steps and around the left side of the house, where a detached garage was located a few dozen feet from the main building. The shadows were darker toward the rear of the property and she had a hard time discerning some of the shapes and objects in the back yard. She was nearing the back corner of the house when she thought she heard a muffled cry. She immediately dropped to her left knee and whipped her pistol out of the holster.

Amy's heart pounded in her chest. Although the temperature was dropping with the setting sun, she felt sweat dripping down the back of her neck beneath her blonde ponytail. Gripping her pistol firmly in her hands, she scooted forward, being careful not to make a sound. Before she reached the corner, a figure came into view. She stared for a long second before she realized what she was seeing—a man had his left arm wrapped around the face of a young girl and there was a pistol pushed against her right temple. The girl tried to talk, but the inside crook of the man's elbow was smothering her.

The man didn't immediately see Amy squatting there pressed up against the house, so she remained motionless as he looked toward the front yard. When he turned his attention back toward the garage, Amy eased her left hand to her belt and turned down the volume on her radio. *All I need is for someone to call out on the radio right now,* she thought, wondering how she was going to get the word out that she needed backup.

The girl struggled against the man's control, but he easily pushed her forward. He whispered a warning for her to keep moving and stay quiet or he would shoot her in the head.

Amy trained her front sight on the back of the man's head, right at the base of the skull. She thought about shooting him, but she was worried he would flinch and pull the trigger, killing the young girl. Rising slowly to her feet, she moved deeper into the yard until she was directly behind the man and about twenty-five feet away from him. She would freeze each time he'd turn his head toward the front yard, and then wait until he started moving again. She mirrored his movements, trying to get closer to him as he reached the door of the garage, but she was still too far away to do anything.

The man turned his head as he reached for the doorknob and Amy froze, but it was too late. Her movement must've caught his eye, because he whelped and quickly whirled around. He pushed the girl between him and Amy. "Get back or I'll kill her!" he said, his voice laced with fear and desperation. "I swear to God, I'll do it!"

"Whoa," Amy said, steadying her pistol with both hands. "No one has to die."

"She's going to die if you don't back away!"

"You can't do that," Amy said calmly. She wanted to let go of the pistol with her left hand so she could key up her radio. She needed to alert her office somehow and she needed backup, but she dared not give up her two-handed grip. "You can't shoot her."

The man's face twisted in contempt. "And why the hell not?"

"First off, she's your daughter. Second, if you shoot her, I shoot you…a lot," Amy said simply. "And you don't want to be shot today."

"How do you know what I want?"

"If you wanted to be shot you would've come through the front door guns-a-blazing, but you didn't." Amy shook her head. "No, sir; instead, you decided to make a run for it. That tells me you're a reasonable man. A smart man. Rick—may I call you Rick?"

The man hesitated and Amy realized she'd identified him correctly. The girl had to be Cindy.

"Rick, why don't you take your arm away from Cindy's face? She's having a hard time breathing. You don't want to hurt her."

Rick didn't relax his grip. He began to back toward the door of the garage.

"I can't allow you to enter that garage." Amy's voice was cool and calculating. "If you try to open that door I'm going to be forced to fire on you."

Rick sneered. "You wouldn't dare—not while I'm holding a hostage."

"I wouldn't want to," Amy acknowledged, trying to keep him talking and distracted, "but I'd have to. The book of tactics says so. Once I have you in my sights, I'm supposed to maintain a visual on you."

This seemed to confuse Rick. He licked his dry lips as he tried to decide what to do next. He clearly hadn't anticipated being confronted out in the open. He was about to open his mouth when tires screeched from the street behind Amy. She saw Rick glance in that direction, but she kept her eyes on him, hoping it was her backup, and not someone he knew.

"Who is it, Rick?" Hoping it was Susan or Clint, Amy raised her voice to alert them to her location. "What do you see?"

"I don't see anything, but if it's more of your people, I'm going to end this once and for all."

CHAPTER 48

Susan screeched to a halt and jumped out of her Tahoe. I slipped from the passenger seat and we made our way toward the house in a crouching run. Susan suddenly shoved her arm toward me and stopped me in my tracks. Pressing her soft lips to my ear, she asked me if I'd heard voices.

I shook my head. It was growing darker by the minute, but we could see each other in the glow from the nearby streetlight.

She shot a thumb toward the garage we'd searched last Friday. "I heard Amy's voice back there." She then pointed toward the opposite side of the house, where the carport was located. "I'll make my way around the house on that side and come up behind them."

I nodded and headed toward the corner of the house nearest the garage. When I peeked around the house, I sucked in my breath. Rick had an arm around Cindy's face and an old revolver pushed up against her head. Amy was standing near the house and had her pistol trained on Rick.

I needed Rick's attention focused toward the front of the house so Susan could get behind him. There was an oak tree between the house and the garage and I quickly stepped toward it, calling out as I did so. "Rick, this is Clint Wolf, what's going on over here?"

Rick turned to face me, spinning Cindy around and used her as a shield. "Stay back! I'm warning you—if either of you take a step toward me, I'm going to kill her."

This was all too familiar and I had to blink away my past. *Focus, Clint,* I thought as I steadied my gun hand against a tree branch. I placed my front sight over Rick's right eye. He was about ten yards away, which would be an easy shot with my Beretta, but a handgun round would not produce an instantaneous no-reflex kill shot. As long as the muzzle of his revolver was pressed against Cindy's head, we'd have to try negotiating with him.

Amy turned quickly to glance at me and I gave her a nod. She'd established initial contact with Rick, so it would be best if she continued talking to him. I just needed him watching me so he wouldn't see Susan, who had melded into the tree line behind his house and was making her way through the dark shadows toward the back of the garage. I couldn't really see her, but every now and then the lights from the street glinted off her gold badge.

"Why don't you tell us why you're doing this?" Amy asked. "Whatever it is you're going through, we can help. I know it might seem like the end of the world right now, but it's not. You can move past this."

"I'm not going to prison." Rick shuffled closer to the garage. "I'm going to get in my car and I'm going to drive out of here with Cindy. As long as you guys stay out of the way, no one will get hurt."

"We can't let you leave," Amy said. "I already told you—it's in the rule book. We're not allowed to let you go mobile, so you've got to work with us here. Maybe you can leave Cindy with us and leave on your own."

"You really think I'm that stupid?" He scoffed. "The second I let go of her you're going to shoot me. That's also in the rule book, isn't it?"

"There's another way." Amy kept her eyes focused like a laser on Rick as Susan slid along the side of the garage. Susan's pistol was out and it was pointing directly at the back of Rick's head.

"The only way this ends well is if you two back off and let me leave." Rick's voice was growing increasingly desperate. "If no one tries to follow me, I'll let Cindy go when I reach the parish line. If I see anything that even resembles a cop car…she's going to die."

"That's your daughter we're talking about," Amy said. "You can't be serious."

"Look at her." Rick spat the words. "She looks nothing like me. I'm no more her dad than I am Burton's."

I saw Cindy's eyes widen and then narrow in anger. I cocked my head sideways as I studied the part of her face that wasn't covered by Rick's hairy arm. Her face was contorted and she was shifting her feet. I didn't realize what she was doing until Rick cried out in pain and tried to jerk his arm away from her face, but her teeth were clamped tightly to his flesh.

Sensing she had an opportunity to escape, Cindy ducked low and broke free from Rick's grasp. She lurched forward and ran toward Amy, who dropped her pistol so it wasn't pointing at Cindy. I didn't have a shot on him either, so I moved toward my left, trying to get clear of Cindy. Susan was quickly closing the gap between them, but Rick's gun hand was coming up too fast. I still didn't have a shot because Susan was in my cross-fire. I hollered a warning toward Amy just as his gun went off.

In my peripheral vision, I saw Amy dive toward Cindy and crash into her. They both hit the ground hard. I couldn't tell if one or both of them were hit and I still couldn't risk a shot for fear of hitting Susan, so I rushed forward to place myself in front of Cindy and Amy.

Susan's movements were a blur in the dim light from the street. She stepped to Rick's right and jumped into the air, executing a front kick to the back of his right elbow. Bones crunched as the inside crook of his elbow shot upward, leaving his gun hand behind. The fingers of his right hand went limp and the revolver dangled in mid-air. I continued moving forward, but Susan delivered a lightning-fast roundhouse kick that caught the revolver in mid-air and slammed it into the side of Rick's head. He fell to the ground in a heap.

While Susan cuffed him, I rushed to help Cindy off the ground. "Are you hurt?" I asked.

Trembling, she shook her head. "I'm...I'm okay."

Amy bounced to her feet and dusted off her shirt, then pushed up beside me to check Cindy for bullet holes. "Are you sure you're okay?"

"Yes, ma'am."

I looked Amy over. "And you?"

She nodded. "I'm fine."

I walked to where Susan was cuffing Rick. His right arm was bent in the wrong direction, but he was unconscious and didn't seem to notice. I pulled out my cell phone and squatted to take a picture of the revolver on the ground. Amy joined me and held out a pair of latex gloves she'd removed from a pouch on her belt.

After donning the gloves, I lifted the revolver and checked the alignment of the cylinder—it was off. "This is the murder weapon," I said, opening the cylinder to unload it. I made a mental note of the position of the spent casing and removed the five live rounds first.

"I didn't murder anyone," said a groggy Rick, who was now semi-alert and being helped to his feet by Susan. Blood poured freely from a nasty gash on the side of his head. "Never saw that gun in my life."

Susan held him steady with one hand and advised him of his Miranda rights. Before she could finish, he said he already knew his rights.

"I want my lawyer, bitch," Rick said. "I ain't saying a word to you or any other pig until I see one."

My blood instantly boiled at the way he spoke to Susan, but I didn't say a word. Susan was very capable of defending herself, but—like every good cop—she wasn't fazed by the suspect's comments. As for me, I could handle the worst of insults with the best of them, but I knew I was going to have a hard time hearing them hurled at the woman I loved. I was just hoping those instances would be rare.

Susan took Rick by the arm and indicated with her head for him to walk toward the front of the house. When she touched his arm, he cried out in pain. He began complaining about police brutality and threatening to sue the office. As he spoke, his words were drawn and slurred and blood continued to drain from his head, where a large lump had formed. I wondered if he might be suffering from a brain injury. He looked deranged, like something from out of *The Walking Dead*.

"Just keep walking," Susan told him. "If I have to carry you, it'll hurt a lot worse."

After asking Amy to keep an eye on the house until I could secure a search warrant, Cindy and I followed Susan to her Tahoe and I watched as she pulled out a first aid kit and bandaged Rick's head before securing him in the back seat on the passenger side. I told Cindy to ride in the front with Susan and I sat beside Rick. Since he'd invoked his right to counsel, I couldn't question him, but there was a lot I wished I could ask him. I was just hoping Judith was willing to talk now that Cindy was safe.

While I was fairly certain the revolver in Rick's possession was the one that had killed Fowler Underwood, I needed more evidence to prove he was the one who actually killed the old mountain man. Since he had lawyered up, I would be forced to rely on Judith to fill in the missing pieces to this crime puzzle. Question was: would she do it? And if she did turn on him, how reliable would her testimony be? She had already lied to me, so I would need to corroborate every little thing she told me…if I could.

CHAPTER 49

Melvin met us in the parking lot when Susan and I arrived at the police department with Rick and Cindy.

"Ride with me to the hospital," Susan told Melvin, "so Clint can interview Judith Vincent."

"You'd better not badger her!" Rick said, sounding like a drunken man. "I'll sic my lawyer on you so fast your head will explode."

Since Rick initiated contact with me after invoking his right to an attorney, I decided to use that opportunity to plant a seed of doubt in his mind. "Judith's already given me enough information to put Rick away for the rest of his life," I said to Susan. "Next, we'll start working on our case for the death penalty."

"That's bullshit." Rick's head swayed from side to side as though it were going to fall off his shoulders. "She would never betray me. You'd better do what she says and get her a lawyer before you—"

"Sorry," I said before Melvin slammed the back door, "but you've already asked for *your* lawyer, so we're done here."

Susan gave me a wink as she drove away and I just stood watching until her taillights had almost reached the intersection with Main and Washington, lost in thought as I tried to put the pieces together before meeting with Judith.

"Mister Clint?" Cindy asked in a low voice. "Are we going inside?"

I snapped my head around and apologized. "Let's go inside and let your mom know you're okay."

We trudged up the concrete steps and Cindy stopped at the landing, turned to face me. "Did my dad kill Troy?"

I frowned. "I'm not sure, but I'll let you know as soon as I know."

She stood looking up at me for a long moment, and then finally turned away.

I held the door for her and watched as she ran into Judith's open arms. The two embraced while Cindy excitedly told her mom what had happened back at the house. Judith clung tightly to Cindy and cried, thanking God that she was okay. At one point, she looked over Cindy's shoulder and said, "Thank you so much for keeping my baby safe."

I only nodded. I didn't want to rush them, but I wanted to know what information she possessed. Finally, Judith wiped her eyes and told Cindy she had to talk with me alone.

"You can sit in the dispatcher's office," I offered Cindy. "Burton's in there right now."

I saw Cindy's eyes cloud over at the mention of Burton. "Is it true? He's not really my brother?"

As much as she had seemed to dislike Burton, she was genuinely sad. Judith melted into Cindy and cried some more. "My dear girl, he is, and will always be, your brother—and don't you ever doubt that again."

"Come on, Mrs. Vincent," I said, coaxing her along. "Let's get this settled so y'all can go home as a family."

She wiped her eyes and nodded. "Go wait with Burton, dear," she said to Cindy, and then followed me through the lobby door on the right and down the hall to the interview room.

"So, where were we?" I asked once we were seated.

"The last thing you asked me about was my work."

I pulled out my notepad and nodded. "But let's start from the beginning."

"How far back?" she asked, blowing her nose into a Kleenex.

"Eighteen years...back to when Larry Cooper was murdered."

"I already told you that I don't know anything about that. I met Rick when he was—"

"I know what you told me," I said, interrupting her. "I want you to start over, but this time I want you to tell me the truth."

She blinked twice. "But I am."

I folded my arms across my chest. "A curious thing...Rick didn't want me badgering you."

"Okay. And...?"

"He seemed confident you hadn't told on him and he said you would never betray him. This makes me believe y'all had a plan, and he was worried I'd break you down and get you to confess if I badgered you."

"He threatened Cindy, and that's why he believes I haven't said anything. He knows I would rather die than let anything bad happen to my kids."

"You just said *kids*—plural. I thought Burton wasn't your child."

"He's not my biological son, but I raised him since he was small, so he's like a son to me."

I nodded slowly. "So, you started to tell me it was all Rick—that he was responsible for the murders."

Judith fixed me with her big brown eyes, as though trying to determine how much she should tell me.

"Look, Mrs. Vincent, a few seconds ago you said you'd rather die than let anything bad happen to your kids." I pause to let her ponder what I'd just said. "Did you mean it or was it a load of crap?"

"I meant it."

"Then why don't you tell me what happened? And why don't you start from the beginning?"

"All I know is Rick killed that stranger because he was snooping around asking questions. Rick was worried he'd find out the truth about Burton not being his son."

I shook my head. "Rick already knew Burton wasn't his son. You both knew that." I leaned my forearms on the desk. "Look, sometimes we have to do things we don't want to do, but it's necessary. And by *things*, I mean sometimes we have to kill people who deserve killing. It's not something we want to do and we certainly didn't sign up for it, but sometimes we just have to do it."

"I don't know what you're talking about."

"Well, let's go over what I know. Firstly, I know you're Melissa Cooper. Secondly, I know Burton is Drake Cooper. Thirdly, I know Larry Cooper is Burton's dad and, lastly, I know you killed Larry because he was beating on you. Like I said, sometimes we have to kill people who deserve killing, and we're often justified in doing so. It's lying about it that makes it seem wrong."

After staring at me for a long moment, Judith finally took a breath and let out a long sigh. "You're only right about two things. I *am* Melissa Cooper and I *did* kill Larry because he was beating on me, but you're wrong about the rest."

CHAPTER 50

"Wait a minute," I said. "If you're Melissa Cooper, then Burton has to be Drake."

Judith—well, Melissa—shook her head and frowned.

"Ma'am, I need you to explain what's going on here—and I want the truth. If Burton isn't Drake, then where is Drake?"

"Drake's dead." Tears flowed down Melissa's cheeks again. "One of the bullets meant for Larry struck Drake in the stomach and he died three days later."

I was confused, but I didn't let her know it. "So, the bullet that went through the wall struck Drake while he was in his crib?"

Melissa's head jerked upward. "How'd you know that?"

"I saw the crime scene photographs and figured it out." I leaned forward and studied Melissa closely. "You killed your own son?"

She scrubbed at the tears on her face and nodded. "It was my idea—to kill Larry—and I'll regret that decision for the rest of my life. Rick and I had been talking behind Larry's back and Rick knew about the beatings." She paused to take a trembling breath. "Rick told me he loved me one night on the phone and he wanted me to leave Larry. He promised to take me away and keep me safe, but I knew Larry would eventually track me down and kill me and Drake." She shuddered. "He was always threatening to hurt Drake if I didn't do what he told me to do. I knew the only way to truly escape was to kill Larry, and I told Rick I was going to do it with or without him."

When she was silent for a long time, I asked her to go on.

She blew her nose on a Kleenex and continued. "Rick and Larry had known each other for years and Rick had supplied Larry with heroin on a few occasions—it's actually how I met Rick for the first time. Anyway, Rick told Larry he could get him a shipment of heroin from out of town, but he would need his usual ten percent up front. When he told Larry it would be five hundred thousand dollars worth of heroin, Larry went on a stealing spree to raise the money.

"Once Larry had raised the fifty grand, he called Rick and told him to bring over the drugs. When Larry usually conducts his business, I go to the back bedroom. This time, I hung around the kitchen while they were talking. When Larry stuffed the packages of drugs in his gym bag and Rick had the money, I walked up and fired a shot at Larry." She stopped and shook her head, tears flowing down her face. "I missed and Larry jumped to his feet. I freaked out and fired again and again. I kept firing even after the gun was empty and Rick had to stop me."

After another long pause, I asked her to continue.

"When Rick took the gun away from me, I went to grab Drake so we could leave. I'd already packed our clothes and had stashed them under the bed. I went for the clothes first. Drake was crying and I thought it was because of the loud noise, but then I saw the blood on his stomach." She squeezed her eyes shut, as though doing so would block the image from her mind. "I wrapped him in his blankets and ran to the car. I wanted to take him to a hospital but Rick said we would both go to jail and I'd never see him again."

I scowled, wondering how selfish a mother would have to be to place her freedom before the life of her child. She appeared tormented enough by the memory of what she'd done, so I left it alone. Instead, I asked what they did when they left the trailer.

"We were both scared and didn't know what to do, so we fled the state. We came to his parents' house and hid Drake in the barn."

"What'd y'all do with Drake when he died?"

"We buried him behind Rick's dad's house." She scrubbed a stream of tears from her face. "I still go there and visit him. He was my first child and I know God punished me for killing Larry. I swore I would never do another bad thing in my life, because bad things truly do come back to haunt you."

I remembered something Burton had told me. "Well, if this is all true and your dad is Fowler Underwood, why does Burton think your parents live in Upper Chateau?"

"Because that's what I told him."

I stared blankly at her and was about to ask who the imposters were when she waved me off.

"I told Burton my dad died when I was a teenager and my mom died when he was a baby," she explained. "He's never met them, but

I told him they were from Upper Chateau. There's even this house outside of town that I've always thought was beautiful, and I told him it was where they lived when they were alive."

I nodded my understanding, feeling sorry for Burton. He'd been lied to his entire life. I couldn't imagine my life being turned upside down. I pulled the flyer from my file and stared at the picture of Drake. It sure looked a lot like Burton. And the DNA results concluded Burton was related to Larry.

"So," I began slowly, "you must've been pregnant with Burton when Drake was killed. Isn't that right?"

She nodded her head.

"Did Larry know?"

"No. I didn't even know until later, after we were in Louisiana for a few weeks."

I considered this new information for a moment, wondering what Rick knew and when he knew it. I pursed my lips. "You made Rick believe Burton was his kid, didn't you?"

Melissa hesitated, then nodded.

"He knows better now. How'd he find out?"

"I told him. I figured it'd be better coming from me than from some DNA test you were conducting."

I grunted. "So, Burton told you?"

"He tells me everything—even things I don't want to know. Rick was so angry. He threatened to leave me, but then I threatened to expose what he'd done, so we were both stuck with each other."

I stared deep into Melissa's bloodshot eyes. Not only had this woman allowed her baby to die, but she remained with the man who had killed her own father. Although her pretty face appeared innocent and sweet, she was far from either. "How could you stay with the man who killed your father? I understand that what happened to Drake was an accident, but your dad was deliberately shot six times in the back. How could you stay with Rick, and then lie for him?"

"He didn't kill my dad."

"Then who did?"

"No one."

My brow furrowed. "What are you talking about?"

"My dad's not dead."

I scoffed. "The dead guy in the canal was identified as Fowler Underwood—unless you're now saying Fowler Underwood wasn't your dad."

"Fowler Underwood is my dad"—Melissa shook her head

slowly—"but it wasn't him in the canal."

"Okay," I said, deciding to play along, "if it wasn't your dad, then who was he?"

"It was Sheriff Burns from Blackshaw County."

CHAPTER 51

My mind whirled as Melissa explained. Fowler had been tearing Sheriff Burns' wanted posters down for years. When Burns—now retired, thanks to his attack on Fowler—saw the flyers that Fowler's siblings had put up around town, he decided it was time for some payback. He went around town changing the contact information on all of the missing person flyers from Fowler's number to his own. So, when Kegan had called the number on the poster, he actually reached Sheriff Burns, who decided the best way to redeem himself was to be proven right about Melissa and to bring her to justice once and for all.

One of Melissa's cousins on her mom's side had overheard Burns bragging in a Birchtown bar about how he'd received a tip from Louisiana about Melissa's whereabouts. He said he called the number a hundred times until someone finally answered and told him where the tip had originated.

"The best part," Burns had said belligerently, "is everyone will think I'm Fowler." He showed off some homemade "private eye" business cards he had made in Fowler's name and said he was heading to Louisiana the next day. "I'm going to bring back the head of Melissa Cooper and drop it on the doorsteps of the sheriff's department," he had been heard declaring. "See if they call me crazy then!"

"Wait a minute," I said, interrupting Melissa's story. "The man we found in the canal wore a belt buckle with your dad's initials cut into the underside. And your brother even confirmed that your dad was the one who tracked you down through the phone calls."

Melissa smiled. "Detective Wolf, would you lie to protect

someone you love?"

As I pondered her question, she continued telling me how her cousin had notified her dad about what she'd heard in the bar, and her dad immediately called to warn her. "It was the first time I'd heard from him since I left," she said, weeping softly. "Back then, he told me I could never contact him because there were warrants for my arrest and he knew Sheriff Burns would never quit until he found me. Boy was he right."

"How'd Rick kill Burns?"

"The school called to tell us a man had come by showing a picture that looked like Burton, so we knew he was here. That same Thursday, Cindy said she saw a strange truck down the street and we figured he had found us. Rick stayed home from work the next day to see if the truck would return, and it did." The more she spoke, the stronger her voice became. "That's when he killed him. It was the first time he'd killed anyone and it made him crazy. I...he's scary to be around now. I really think he's a danger to me and my children."

"How'd he do it?" I asked again.

"He followed the truck to the end of the street in my Jeep and blocked him in. Sheriff Burns got out and walked over carrying one of the flyers—the same kind that Burton clipped to the refrigerator—and he asked Rick if he'd seen Drake or me. He identified himself as my dad. Rick told him he was trespassing and that he needed to leave the neighborhood or he would call the local police. They exchanged words and Burns turned angrily to walk back to his truck." She sighed. "Rick stepped out of my Jeep and shot him in the back. He had no choice, you know?"

I waved off her last comment. "Continue, please."

"He dragged the sheriff's body through the woods and dumped him in the canal. He then hid the blue truck in our garage and burned all of his credentials in the fire pit, along with one of his shoes that had fallen off when Rick was dragging his body."

I studied Melissa with hard eyes. "Would it surprise you to know that I actually met with Sheriff Burns in Tennessee three days ago?"

"Not at all," Melissa said coolly. "But you weren't speaking to Sheriff Burns...you were speaking to my dad."

"Right...well, you still never explained why Sheriff Burns was wearing a belt buckle with your dad's initials carved into the back of it."

"There are a thousand buckles like that with his initials carved into them," Melissa said. "My dad makes them and sells them. His initials are his brand. And everyone who knows my dad knows that's the only buckle he ever wears, so I'm sure the sheriff went out and bought one to convince people he was my dad." She huffed. "Did you check the buckle my dad was wearing when you went to Burns' cabin? Because that one has his initials on it too."

I hadn't, but I did remember how Moe Cooper claimed he spoke with Fowler on the twenty-third of September. When I'd questioned him, he reconsidered, but it turns out the man was correct. Fowler was laying down a reverse alibi.

"What about Troy Gandy?" I asked.

Melissa's shoulders sagged. "I still can't believe Rick killed that poor kid."

I asked her what happened and she said Rick heard a noise outside one night and went to investigate. "He found Troy snooping around the back yard. When Rick hollered at him, Troy ran to the back of the garage. Rick caught up to him and they started fighting near a bicycle." Tears began to flow again. "Rick said he thought Troy saw the blue truck through the window, so he had no choice but to silence him."

"He strangled him?" I asked.

She nodded. "He said he used a chain or wire from the bicycle. It was so horrible. I almost turned him in right then, but he told me I'd go to prison for killing Larry. When I said I didn't care about that, he said he'd hurt my kids. He knows Larry used to control me by threatening to hurt Drake, and he began to do the same thing. It was so horrible."

I drummed my fingers on the desk. "We searched the garage Friday night but didn't find the truck."

"Rick moved it while I was here with Burton and Cindy. He didn't tell me where he moved it, but when I got home he said it was done, that we were all in the clear now. He said we should go on about our daily lives and just act normal. He promised me it would all blow over and we'd never be caught."

That's what they all think. I glanced down at my notes.

"We recovered a black revolver from Rick when we arrested him earlier tonight," I said. "Would that be the same handgun you used to kill Larry?"

Melissa nodded. "I hadn't seen it for years after Rick took it from me the night I…you know, shot Larry, but I saw it yesterday. I asked Rick what he was doing with it, because I had told him to get rid of it eighteen years ago. He told me he buried it with Drake, but that was a lie. Everything he ever told me was a lie."

CHAPTER 52

I went over Melissa's story in my head and asked a few follow-up questions. I'd need to corroborate her story with her job and I needed to search the fire pit at her house. We'd recovered fingerprints from the body in the morgue, so those would have to be compared against the Blackshaw County Sheriff's Department employee records for Sheriff Burns. If they didn't match, I'd have to compare his DNA against Melissa's to make sure he wasn't Fowler. And once the ballistics came back on the gun we recovered from Rick Vincent, we'd know for sure if it was used to kill Larry Cooper and Sheriff Burns.

"Am I going to jail?" Melissa's voice broke through my thoughts. "If you lock me up, what's going to happen to Cindy and Burton?"

I sighed. "If what you're telling me is true, you didn't have a hand in killing anyone in my town, so I don't have a reason to arrest you."

"What about...um—"

"Larry?" I pursed my lips and stared thoughtfully at her. "I don't have a warrant from Blackshaw County, but that doesn't mean they don't have one. At some point, I'll have to contact their office and provide them with the information you gave me, but afterward it'll be up to them."

She nodded and asked if she could take Burton and Cindy home. "There's a lot we need to discuss as a family."

"Good luck," was all I could say in support, and then told her I needed her to wait until I'd obtained a search warrant for her property. I also wanted to recover the body of Drake Cooper, so he could get a proper burial, but that would have to come on another day.

After allowing Melissa to sit in the lunchroom with Burton, I typed up the search warrant and then took Cindy's statement while waiting for the judge to sign and return the affidavit and warrant. Once I'd received the judicial authorization, I headed to Dire Lane and searched the Vincent property.

Amidst a pile of melted plastic and burnt wood in the fire pit, I found the remnants of Sheriff Burns' retired law enforcement commission card, a badly charred wallet badge, and the metal arch support from his shoe. When I removed the cover from one of the drums behind the garage, I found that it was filled with nutria traps. I began removing the traps and located a license plate and a badly damaged VIN plate buried halfway down the drum. I called dispatch and requested a license plate check—it came back to a blue Nissan King Cab registered to Sheriff Burns.

Once I was satisfied I'd searched the entire area, I relinquished control of the property back to Melissa and told her I'd be in touch soon. I was going to get with Yates and forward the information I'd uncovered, which might mean I'd be returning to arrest her.

I drove away from the Vincent home and called Susan to let her know what Melissa had said and to describe what I'd found at the house, but she told me she already knew everything. "Rick began spilling his guts while the doctor worked on him," she said. "I tried to tell him to stop, but he just kept talking. I recorded everything on my phone, including me telling him several times that he'd asked for an attorney so I wasn't going to ask him questions. He told me he didn't care, that he was sorry about what he'd done to Cindy and he wanted everyone to know he was responsible for killing the sheriff and Troy."

"What did he say about Larry?"

"He said he and Melissa planned the hit on Larry. He had cooked up some fake drugs and was in the process of selling it to Larry when Melissa opened fire. One stray bullet hit the baby and they panicked. He said they grabbed the infant and the money and high-tailed it out of there. The baby died a few days later and they secretly buried it in his parents' yard in Central Chateau. He said they lived off the money they'd stolen from Larry until Melissa was stable enough to start working." Susan continued telling his story, and it matched Melissa's.

I sighed. Once the lab results came back on the gun, prints, and other evidence we'd submitted, the local case would be a wrap and Rick would be spending the rest of his natural life in prison.

"Oh, and Clint," Susan said, her voice low and somber. "I think I may have messed up."

"What's that?" I asked. "Messed up how?"

She paused for a moment and I could hear her take a deep breath. "I think I broke my leg."

"What?" I nearly dropped my phone. "You're supposed to fight in a couple of weeks!"

"I know," she said. "When I kicked Rick's elbow I felt a shock go up my right leg. It didn't help when I kicked the revolver, and now I've got a lump on my fibula. I'm fixing to go into x-ray."

"I'm on my way." I ended the call and smashed the accelerator. I arrived at the hospital in a record twelve minutes and rushed into the emergency room. Melvin was sitting in the lobby reading a magazine from the nearby rack. He jumped to his feet when I walked in.

"They just took her to x-ray," he said, "but they're thinking it's fractured."

My heart sank. She wanted this fight more than anything and she would be devastated if she had to cancel because of an injury. I dropped to the chair beside Melvin and waited...and waited.

Finally, about thirty minutes later, Susan was pushed out in a wheelchair. Her leg was extended straight out and there was a cast around her lower right leg. Her jaw was set and I knew she was angry.

"It's okay," I said when she stood and took the set of crutches from one of the nurses. "I'm sure you'll get another opportunity to fight Ivanov."

Susan didn't say a word as we walked out into the parking lot, and the only sound was that of the crutches clattering against the concrete parking lot. Melvin had stayed behind to wait for the hospital to release Rick, at which time he would transport the murderer to the detention center in northern Chateau.

I reached out to open the door for Susan when we got to my Tahoe. She handed me her crutches and stepped into the passenger seat without much trouble.

"I'm still fighting," she said after I had pulled out of the parking lot and driven a few miles down the road.

"You can't fight!" I stared at her in shock. "You have a broken leg."

"That no one will know about."

I recognized that look in Susan's eyes. There was no use arguing with her. She was going to do what she wanted to do regardless of what I said or did, so the best thing for me to do was just shut up and support her.

CHAPTER 53

8:38 p.m., Saturday, October 29
Houston, Texas

I should've been relaxing. I'd spent the past three weeks working tirelessly to close out the case against Rick, exhume the body of Baby Drake, and help Detective Yates build his case against Melissa.

The coroner had recovered an oblong projectile from the remains of Baby Drake, and after it was compared to the revolver and projectiles from both shootings, we were able to confirm that the revolver was used to kill our canal victim, Larry Cooper, and the infant. The prints from our victim matched the fingerprint card from Sheriff Burns' employment records, confirming he was our canal victim. The blood I'd recovered from the field behind Dire Lane matched the ex-sheriff's DNA, and his toxicology came back clean.

I'd returned to Tennessee and found Fowler Underwood back at his house. He admitted to helping conceal Melissa's crime and tipping them off about Sheriff Burns, but he swore he never intended for Rick to murder his old nemesis. Detective Yates had sworn out a warrant for the arrest of Melissa Cooper and Rick Vincent for killing Larry and shooting Drake, but the authorities there hadn't yet decided what to do with Fowler Underwood for breaking into Sheriff Burns' cabin and posing as the former lawman.

Since Rick was making his way through our court system, Blackshaw County would have to wait their turn, but we had arrested Melissa soon after receiving the warrant, and she was set to be extradited to Tennessee within the week. Burton and Cindy, who were coping just fine, considering all they'd been through, had gone to live with Rick's parents in Central Chateau. I dropped in to see them before leaving for Houston with Susan, and they were adjusting to their new environment.

After all of my hard work, I should've been relaxing and enjoying my time off, but that was difficult to do while I watched the woman I love getting pummeled.

CHAPTER 54

I was sitting at the edge of my seat in the front row nearest the cage, and I was watching Susan trading blows with Antonina Ivanov. Susan looked as focused as I'd ever seen her, and I couldn't help but admire her firm body wrapped in her tight fighting shorts and snug-fitting shirt. Even the blood dripping from her nose looked sexy, but I winced as Ivanov connected with a two-punch combination, snapping Susan's head back.

Damian Conner pounded on the chain-link fence and screamed at Susan to take Ivanov to the ground. "Stop trading with her!" he hollered. "Take her to the ground and finish her!"

Either Susan couldn't hear or she was ignoring him, because she continued to stalk her opponent. Her hands were high in the air as she doggedly moved forward, but it was impossible for her to block all of the Russian fighter's strikes. Immediately after Ivanov delivered another three-punch combination, Susan shot a left round kick to her midsection, followed by an overhand right that seemed to rock Ivanov.

I cheered my approval, but sank back in my chair when Ivanov shot a push kick to Susan's chest that nearly knocked her on her butt. Susan immediately executed a right roundhouse kick to Ivanov's thigh, and she stumbled as she placed her weight back on it.

Although her doctor had advised her not to fight with a cracked fibula, Susan had stubbornly ignored him. After wearing the cast for two weeks, she had removed it herself and began using a compression wrap for support. While she felt the fracture had mended, Damian devised a game plan around her injury and insisted she avoid executing kicks with her right leg. "And I want you to take her down as soon as you get the chance," Damian had instructed. "The quicker it goes to the canvass, the better your chances of beating her."

I'd seen the look in Susan's eyes when he said it and had groaned. I knew right then that she was going to attempt what no fighter had ever accomplished before—she was going to try and beat Antonina Ivanov at her own game and knock out the undefeated Russian. At the moment, it wasn't going so great. Susan had just walked into a straight right hand from Ivanov. It was a power punch that had felled many of her previous opponents, but Susan continued forward. I could tell she was stepping a little gingerly on her right leg and her footwork was not as fluid as it had been earlier.

I glanced to my right, where her mother was seated. Lisa Wilson had her hands up to her face and she jerked each time Susan got hit. Mrs. Wilson was a small-framed woman who was timid and appeared frail. Other than the streaks of white, her hair was the same color as Susan's, and so were her eyes, but that was where the similarities ended for the two women. I didn't know if she would be able to endure watching this brutal slugfest.

The crowd screamed in excitement and I turned just in time to see Susan delivering the last of a punch-kick combination that knocked Ivanov backward into the cage. The Russian fighter lifted her arms as Susan side-stepped to create an angle and then fired off two more punches. Just when I thought she was going to take charge of the bout, the bell rang to end the first round.

I sank back into my chair and ran my fingers through my hair. Damian hurried into the cage with Takecia Gayle, who had agreed to work Susan's corner with him, and they wiped the blood from Susan's face while talking rapidly with her. I could hear Damian pleading with her to take Ivanov to the ground, but Susan didn't respond. She simply stared across the cage in the direction of her opponent. I got the feeling she'd rather die than take the easy way out of the fight, and that scared the crap out of me.

"Is it always like this?" Lisa asked, leaning close and raising her voice to be heard over the crowd. Her chin was shaking and her face was paler than usual. "Does she always get beat this bad?"

I shook my head. "This is the toughest fight of her career."

"Oh, dear," the elderly woman said, wringing her hands and shifting her eyes around the arena. "I don't know how much more of this my heart can take."

"Your daughter's as tough as they come," I said, trying to reassure both of us. "She'll be just fine."

She just nodded and sat on her hands. I looked past her to where Allie and Sammy Boudreaux were sitting, their eyes wide and excited. Susan had obtained complimentary tickets for them to sit at ringside, and it was clearly the highlight of young Sammy's life to that point—maybe even Allie's. Susan had assisted Allie in finding a job and they had located a cozy little apartment that Allie and Sammy could call home. Allie hadn't wanted to return to the home she used to share with Jake. Since the district attorney's office had indicted Jake Boudreaux on charges of attempted first degree murder, she didn't have to worry about him anymore. He would be sitting in jail until his trial, at which time he would go away for at least fifty years. After reviewing the evidence against him and his past criminal record, his attorney was already talking plea deals, but the DA wouldn't agree to anything unless Jake remained in prison until he was too old to hurt anyone again.

As the referee called both women to the center of the ring to begin round two, Damian yelled, "Take her to the ground—for God's sake, do it!"

Susan bit down hard on her mouthpiece and swatted at a stream of blood that had started leaking from her nose. Her jaw was set and her eyes bore straight into Ivanov. I'd seen that look before, and I was suddenly afraid for the Russian.

As soon as the bell rang, Ivanov lunged forward with an overhand right that Susan deftly ducked under. Susan spun around to face Ivanov's back. Instead of taking the Russian to the ground, Susan waited for her to turn.

"Jump on her!" Damian screamed, but his cries were lost in the roar from the crowd, who appreciated Susan's willingness to stand and trade with the legendary striker.

As the two fighters came together, Ivanov landed a wicked left hook to Susan's jaw, but Susan shot a right hand over the hook that landed flush on the Russian's chin. As Ivanov reeled backward out of punching range, Susan switched stances to southpaw and delivered a left roundhouse kick to the Russian's jaw that resounded throughout the arena and brought screaming fans to their feet. Ivanov's hands and head went instantly limp and she fell like a giant tree. When she crashed to the canvass, she lay still.

Still in the moment, Susan charged forward—limping just a little—and had to be nearly tackled by the referee, who spun her away from Ivanov and then dropped to check on the unconscious former champion.

I was on my feet, jumping up and down like a young boy who

had just scored his first homerun. Thin arms wrapped around me and I looked down to see Susan's mom hugging me, tears of joy and relief streaming down her face. I hugged her and looked up. Susan was clinging to the top of the cage pointing in my direction. "I did it!" she screamed. "I actually did it! Now we can start having kids!"

BJ Bourg is a former professional boxer and a lifelong martial artist who hails from the swamps of Louisiana. A thirty-year veteran of law enforcement, he has worked as a patrol cop, a detective, a detective sergeant, a police academy instructor, and the chief investigator for a district attorney's office. He has successfully investigated all types of felony cases and has trained hundreds of law enforcement officers in self-defense, firearms, criminal operations, and many other areas. He retired in October of 2020 and is now a fulltime writer.

Throughout his career, Bourg has served on many specialized units such as SWAT, Honor Guard, the Explosives Search Team, and the Homicide Response Team. He founded his agency's sniper program and served as its leader and instructor for nearly a decade. A graduate of seven basic and advanced sniper schools, he deployed as the primary sniper on dozens of call-outs, including barricaded subjects, hostage rescue operations, and fugitive apprehensions. He also served as the sniper instructor for the 2001 L.T.P.O.A. Conference.

Bourg has been the recipient of numerous awards, including Top Shooter at an FBI Sniper School, the Distinguished Service Medal, and Certificates of Commendation for his work as a homicide detective. In addition to authoring more than forty novels, he has also written dozens of articles for law enforcement magazines, covering a wide range of topics such as defensive tactics, sniper deployment, suspect interrogation, report writing, and more. Above all else, he is a father, husband, and pépère, and the highlight of his life is spending time with his beautiful wife, wonderful children, adorable grandchildren, and German shepherds.

Bourg is originally from Galliano, Louisiana, and he lived most of his life in the Mathews area. He now proudly calls Tellico Plains, Tennessee his home.

Made in United States
North Haven, CT
25 April 2025

68286793R00124